D1023895

MOTHERLUNGE

A NOVEL

KIRSTIN SCOTT

New Issues Poetry & Prose

Western Michigan University
Kalamazoo, Michigan 49008

First American Edition, 2013.

ISBN-13: (paperback) 978-1-936970-11-7

Library of Congress Cataloging-in-Publication Data:
Scott, Kirstin
Motherlunge: A Novel/Kirstin Scott
Library of Congress Control Number: 2012936333

Editor: William Olsen
Managing Editor: Kimberly Kolbe
Layout Editor: Elizabyth A. Hiscox
Cover Design: Lindsey Naylor
Production Manager: Paul Sizer
The Design Center, Gwen Frostic School of Art
College of Fine Arts
Western Michigan University

This book is the winner of the Association of Writers & Writing Programs (AWP) Award for the Novel. AWP is a national, nonprofit organization dedicated to serving American letters, writers, and programs of writing.
Go to www.awpwriter.org for more information.

MOTHERLUNGE

A NOVEL

KIRSTIN SCOTT

NEW ISSUES

 WESTERN MICHIGAN UNIVERSITY

For Bill and Joyce,
Wilhelmina and Oscar,
Sean.

1. WE'LL GET TO NOW LATER

Sometimes, when two people love each other very much, they want to get closer. So they put their bodies as close as possible to each other, like the pages of a book, or two legs inside a mermaid costume. This is called *making love. Having sex.*

Also, come to think of it, *being pregnant.* The fetus nestling against your intestines, bending her ear to the music of digestion....

But we'll get to now later. Right now, I want to talk to you about sex.

2. TWO ON ONE

I lost my virginity under a skylight, under a sweating boy, an arms-length away from a bust of the great inventor, Benjamin Franklin, who from his perch on the nightstand seemed to stare through his spectacles at my recent discovery: a stack of porn magazines, back issues from a previous decade, circa '78. Adam kept them underneath his bed, and while he was down the hall slamming drawers in his parents' bathroom looking for condoms, I'd been reading on a group-sex theme: *Crowd Scenes, Three's Company, Ménage In Gay Paree.* So when Adam, peeling his narrow torso off me, squeaked "Okay?" and finally drove it home, I, like Anonymous, a letter-writing reader from Dayton, OH, thought, *Who would believe this could happen to me? Two on one!*

Evening fell through the skylight, darkening the head and shoulders of our founding father. I bled a little and then stopped. When Adam finally dropped asleep—his lashes batting softly his flushed cheeks—I sat up. I pulled my head and arms through his science fair t-shirt. I put on my glasses, and punched out the extra pillow behind my head. Then I reached under the bed for the December *Oui*, and finished the issue.

I was wearing footies that night—ankle socks with yarn pom-poms behind the heels. I rubbed my footied feet together as I read; lint rose up from my insteps like rice-sized Venuses from the foam. I was seventeen, it was a Friday night in the summer after my senior year, and Adam had said it at last: I was beautiful.

Six days later in a hotel bathroom, my mother found out about Adam and me because I told her. "You are in love," she suggested, jaw in the palms of her hands, dry elbows on her knees as she sat on the toilet. "You are in love with him," she repeated. A garrulous Gemini, my mother's stories tend to puff up, double; eventually everyone is implicated.

"Think!" Dorothy continued, straightening up slowly and pneumatically, "You—my daughter Thea—on the very day your sister is to be married, declare your love for Adam!" In the orange glow from the heat lamp overhead, her tears sparkled like funeral candles on the Mother River Ganges.

"Oh, honey!" My mother began to weep then, slumping forward and wiping her eyes with a wad of toilet paper, then spreading her giant thighs to wipe again. "Oh, oh, oh!" She flushed. Above the crashing surf, her sobs floated up along with her arms, reaching toward me. And in the mirror above the sink, I watched myself bend down to her embrace.

"Oh!" I heard myself repeat. In the circle of her arms I discovered I was crying, too. Is this what love feels like, then, everything growing remote, falling away like objects in the rear view mirror? Panic, relief, regret—it was an hour and a half before Pavia's wedding, and once again I thought of Anonymous: *I'll never forget that hot afternoon.*

We drove to the church, where Walter, our father, stood outside by the front door, smoking and refusing to come in. Thus it was Dorothy—his estranged wife, our mother, two hundred and seventy-eight pounds and giant-moth-like in a sage-colored caftan—who alone compelled Pavia down the aisle and up to the altar. I wasn't wearing my glasses, but I loved the way I knew it would look always, later, on videotape: Pavia's ten attendants ascending on the side to me, the maid of honor and (*yes! yes!*) also the tallest, and across the aisle our tuxedoed escorts—all of us angled like slats of a privacy fence toward the couple on the dais. Rigid in our formal wear, we were a splendid army, serious and duty-bound. The church organ chorded up and down, the congregational infants gurgled. Pavia—beautiful as a bone shard in her plain dress, as evidentiary—turned in her affirmatives; Jack, her groom, sobbingly agreed *I will*. And from behind the tripod, Doug the videographer panned the scene with exquisite Soul Train slowness.

One month later, Adam, sullen after a Saturday teaching AP physics prep courses, failed to comprehend my passion. We were at his house, on the couch; his parents were out of town. I was massaging my third eye with my thumb while we reviewed the newly delivered wedding video.

"See that zoom?" I prompted him, "See that focus on the close up of the bouquet? It's not as easy as it looks." Here Adam made the sound I knew his father—the professor of pure math, acting chair of his department at the U—would make if he were there: a kind of closed-mouth sigh, committed to its single note.

"How about that framing?" I went on to ask. Doug the videographer had tutored me during the wedding reception; I could point out to Adam the way the potted fern flexed in time to the organ's high bronchial melody, how the train of Pavia's dress coiled artfully toward the bridesmaids' shoes. "And what do you make of that filter?" I asked—for indeed the chapel's rosette window strained a shaft of milky light.

"Pavia looks really hot." Adam slid the current *Hustler* off my thigh and settled his head into the center of my Lotus position. This was painful of course—as Dorothy might say, God didn't intend for ankles to bend that much—so I rolled forward into the Cat posture, placing my hands on either side of Adam's bony hips while he sighed again the monotonous sigh he'd inherited from his father. "And so do you, Thea."

"Fine, then," I said, forcing my chin down towards my sternoclavicular joint, breathing into my fourth chakra. My glasses lifted off my nose and hung from my ears; strands of my hair became attracted to the grain of Adam's corduroys. "Fine. You don't think interpretation matters. Well, I don't believe in your stuff either."

"Explain," Adam said, working his hand into my jeans, trawling my underwear.

"That stuff," I said. "Gravity, velocity. Waves, polarity." Evidently my feelings were hurt. So while the air crackled with electricity and the VCR militated for the wedding march (again), I had one more thing to say to the former Merit Scholar—"I mean physical laws, in general"—and I liked the way I said it, daringly, perhaps *huskily*, as if I were dropping objects off some Italian tower, and proving something true. Who could disagree with me, if his zipper were in my teeth? Adam's mouth moved undecidedly, suggesting *oui*. And although our bodies were already in perfect contradiction, Adam had one more thing to ask.

"Sixty-nine?" he said, as if he had his hands in his pockets, and was guessing change by feel alone.

It isn't easy, being novice, and there was love between us (mine). I concluded with remarks that day, quoting "L." and "A." and "Name Withheld" as we enchained a sequence on the rug: the *sopping snatch*; the *throbbing cock*; the *suction* and the *shoot*. In the residence of the math department chair at Rocky Mountain

State, Adam helped me make it up.

So the two of us in love, and also Jack (the groom) and his bride Pavia—add to this seven years. Add a velveting of dust on the wedding video case. Add the fact that Jack and Pavia had moved away to a big city, landed real jobs, bought new cars and a townhouse condo. Add that Jack frequently went away on business and that Adam, now teaching English in Poland through a connection of his father's, wrote me infrequently and signed off "Solidarnosc!" Just thinking about him—the way he never listened to me and was always creepy-quiet during sex—made me mad. "Nyet!" I wrote back. "Dasvidanya!"—a thrilling way to say goodbye forever, I found, before a pogromic loneliness set in.

By then I, too, had gone to college. But of course I was still a waitress. I still lived at home. For me, nothing much had changed except the hostility I felt for the girl who'd lettered ANTHRO, MASS COMM, and GENDER STUD in forward-leaning script on her file cabinet drawers: It grew.

Then, six states away, Pavia suddenly called one night in uncharacteristic distress, saying, "Jack is maybe going. Everything is wrong."

"You go," our mother said, "You go see Pavia." She called up Walter and they bought me a plane ticket. I packed some clothes in Dorothy's yellow vinyl suitcase. I zipped it shut and buckled the silver belt around its middle, sensing that this suitcase—the one that would accompany me on my first trip to the big city—was as quaint as a hairnet, as a sanitary belt, as a can of aerosol hairspray. I didn't care; I was on my way. On the plane I had a window seat. I watched my hometown sink away and all the rest of the country rise into view, curving in front of me at last, expectant.

When I got off the plane, there was Pavia with a paperback copy of *In Search of Excellence*, dressed in what I recognized as sportswear. You know the drill—the way she quickly counted the crowd, looking for me; the way she smiled and waved. The way we hugged, the way young women struggle with luggage that isn't really all that heavy. That habit of apologizing about the interior of a car, for all that customized debris—the gum wrappers and empty drink cups, the dog-eared stack of papers from work that need to be moved off the passenger's seat to make room for you.

I had scarcely seen Pavia since her wedding day, and she did seem changed; time showed. Unwinding the car down the parking structure's nauseating ramp, steering hard left, my older sister— eyebrows meeting in a new vertical wrinkle, teeth indenting lower lip—had never looked so determined while doing a simple thing, nor more lovely. She flung her change at the fee attendant in a gesture of release, pressed firmly on the gas, and we were off.

Our mother had always told us that a headache is a sign of fear, a sign of turning away from the Reality of Love. Somewhere high above the khaki plains of the Midwest, I had developed a headache that day, bad. But I was having it as surrogate I thought, for my sister and the imminent loss of Jack, about which we'd been quiet.

I personally hadn't turned away from shit, I told myself. For it was only a few months before, I privately recalled, that I'd pried Adam's skinny thighs apart, begging *baby, let me in!* Love—I reassured myself that day, pressing firmly on the flesh between my thumb and index finger, seeking acupressure's indirect relief—*Love; I want it.* But meanwhile we drove on in silence, both windows open in Pavia's two-door coupe, the safety straps slapping out a happy rhythm on our similar sets of breasts.

There was traffic as we got closer to the city. Our lane moved slowly toward the gleaming prisms of the downtown buildings, fake-seeming and impressive; TV helicopters hung above us like sci-fi insects. Would we ever get to Pavia's house,

I wondered? My headache throbbed against my eyeballs and my earlier sense of purpose—vague yet galvanizing—drained away as through a shunt. What was I doing there? I squeezed the chi point again and took a cleansing breath.

"We're halfway," Pavia told me, turning up the radio, "We're halfway there, almost home," and these fractions were the only topic between us as Pavia bisected again and again the distance we had left to go—one-quarter, one-eighth, one-sixteenth—for Pavia was always good at math, and she knew that I was in pain. And finally, defying calculation, we did arrive.

Outside Pavia's townhouse, a Great Dane was standing up with his wide brown paws hooked over the top of the wrought-iron fence. In the words of Anonymous, *it was an incredible day!*—Pavia all at once asking of me: how was Dad, how was Mom, how was—what's his name?— Adam?—as we dragged our mother's ugly yellow suitcase to the gate.

It was there, in a scene reminiscent of the docks and railroad platforms, with a plastic bag waving from the stop sign and maple seeds unscrewing in the air all around us, that I was introduced to Pavia's guard dog, General. I had my arm around my sister, who suddenly was talking like a child.

"General?" Pavia whined, stooping down and covering her kneecaps with her hands, "General? Say hello to Thea."

Pavia pulled her hand along his bony back. I held out my left wrist, but General pushed it away with a vigorous thrust of his two wet nostrils. He sunk his nose into my crotch. And then I was laughing, but my sister was apologizing, while General nodded his head up and down.

3. SOMETHING IN THE WAY

When it's time to have The Talk with your daughter, you find
there's something in the way, a meaning. So much genitourinary
detail, the act's unlikely biomechanics, the euphemisms for all
of the above plus the apparent lack of motive—all this merely
straddles, like a teen movie's unprepared coed newly atop the
mechanical bull, a simple message: *Be careful. Please, please be
careful.*

Can we ever get around it? Are we ever done saying that?
I should warn you: I'm only getting started.

4. LOVE IS DEAF

It was the night before my father, seventeen years old, left to drive up north to start college. It was dinnertime, and he was sitting at the fleck-topped linoleum table waiting for potatoes. A napkin fluttered on the thigh of the leg he was jiggling up and down. Meanwhile his father, sitting across the table, slowly closed his *Popular Science* and laid it to his right, at the three o'clock position.

"Walter," my father's father said, his eyes hard under his tangled eyebrows, "Be careful. Take care of your genetic material." He lifted the saltshaker and shook it over his pot roast in long, decisive downstrokes.

"I know you know what I mean," he shook, now looking down at his meat. "Be careful when you start taking girls out. Be careful *how* you date. *Who* you date."

My father's mother came into the dining room holding a casserole dish between two quilted oven mitts. She'd been humming to show she was busy, but she stopped as she leaned over the back of Walter's chair.

"*Whom* you date," she corrected, shifting the dish to one

hand, gripping the serving spoon with the other. Then she spoke more softly, straight into Walter's ear. "The important thing,"—Walter felt her breath right there—"is to *never* make fun of the fat girls."

It's the last piece of advice my father remembers her giving; she died of a stroke one month afterwards.

"Fat girls have feelings," she had continued that night, her face flushing with heat or undiagnosed hypertension, "*Deep* feelings—and often the best personalities." While the serving spoon she held aloft steamed up her son's glasses, she waited until Walter turned his face toward her and gave her a foggy, grateful smile. She beamed back at him and flicked au gratin potatoes onto his plate with a heavy, punctuating glop.

Recounting this last supper, Walter always reminded Pavia and me that his mother wasn't fat herself. In the black and white photo he keeps on his dresser, we can see it's true: she was tall, celery-like; she stands in the backyard with one pale and stringy forearm shading her eyes from the sun. Neither was she jolly; she was stern-seeming in a folk-art way, reassuring—she seems to press back the tattered cornstalks that start at the yard's edge and go on through the gray, flat horizon of central Idaho, the end. "Disciplined," my father has called her, discipline being something he admires and has mostly managed to avoid in his life, starting with college. Because Walter went to college that first semester, and even before his mother died he'd met a girl—chubby, sexy Dorothy—and perhaps overdoing things a bit in terms of good will toward the overweight, had gotten her pregnant.

Dorothy's deep feelings about this development were happy ones. Being pregnant made her feel calm for the first time in her life. How could there be a bad decision when she felt so peaceful, so special? She felt like someone perfectly cast as the slave girl in a Bible movie—regal in her scented scarves, the coins on her bra winking in the lamplight of the desert tent—chosen to bear the chosen child, *Ah, Abraham!* So when Walter reflexively proposed marriage, squeezing her fingers together painfully as they walked through the campus quadrangle one night, she accepted right away. And when Walter began to cry, Dorothy pulled his head to what she thought of as her *bosom*. This was the time before breasts were individualized, and her bosom therefore was a singular characteristic, a fatty integrant over her evenly beating heart.

"It's fine," she told him, rubbing her cheek on the gristle of his crew cut. "It's fine. You'll be fine."

This, it turned out and in fulfillment of the cliché, was just the hormones talking. Once Dorothy and Walter were married (a Christmas wedding, Methodist) and the baby arrived (weeks early, a furry four-pound girl, Pavia), it gradually became clear that things were not fine. Walter was still in school, working part-time stocking shelves at a grocery store, drinking a 6-pack on his walk home to the apartment every night. Dorothy stayed in bed with the baby all day and night. The phone would ring and ring and ring; she wouldn't pick it up. Most of the time it would be Dorothy's mother, Alva, on the line.

Thus, for example, it was midnight and the phone was ringing. Walter let himself in the locked door of the apartment, suppressing an elastic, malty burp as he picked up the phone.

"Hello?"

"Put her on," Alva said. Walter could hear his mother-in-law windexing something in the background, a high nervous squeak. "Aren't you supposed to be at work?"

"I just came in the door. I think Dorothy's asleep."

"I've been ringing all day and no one's picking up." The windexing stopped; my grandmother was waiting.

"Dorothy's here. She's fine," Walter said. The phone had a long cord, and he had pulled it behind him as he stepped into the bedroom. He turned the light on and watched Dorothy roll over in their bed and look up at him. The room smelled like the back of the dairy aisle at work, where spilled milk and lint from the refrigerator grills made a sour felt on the floor.

My mother? Dorothy mouthed the question to Walter: her face wrinkled up as if she'd been pinched. She shook her head— *No!*—as she sat up and reached for the baby.

"Alva? She's nursing the baby now, okay? She'll call you later."

Walter walked back to hang up the phone on the little table by the front door, then returned to lean against the frame of the bedroom door. He watched Dorothy open up her robe and lean forward. One blue-veined breast swung free over the baby like a dirigible emerging from low cloud cover. *Oh the humanity!* The baby, my sister Pavia of course, began a raspy, burning scream.

"When did she last have a bottle?" Walter asked.

Dorothy pouted. "I don't know," she said, and she applied the baby to her nipple as you would hang a picture to a wall hook. "Anyway, I want to keep breastfeeding. Keep trying, I mean." She winced a little as Pavia slid off her breast.

"Alva said she was calling all day." Dully, Walter watched Dorothy try again. Now Dorothy was pressing the baby's dark-haired head into her left breast like a failing nametag. "You slept a lot again? What about Pavia?"

Dorothy set her soft mouth in a hard line. "Dr. Keller says that it can take several weeks before breastfeeding is well established. You've got to keep at it and get plenty of rest."

"But Jesus Christ, Dorothy." Once again, the baby failed to adhere and now Walter felt the air thicken with the sound of her bleating cry; it sifted like a damp powder through the room. He was suddenly very sorry he'd finished all the beer he'd taken from the store that night.

"You've got to give her a bottle," he said. "She's probably dehydrated." Walter had already abandoned the pre-medical coursework he'd started with, but he'd had a semester of human biology—and anyone who'd ever tended a houseplant would see the problem here.

Dorothy looked down at the baby. She stuck a dimpled index finger into the baby's mouth where strands of spit draped the gums like cobwebs.

"Well, you get her a bottle then." Dorothy handed the baby to Walter straight-armed, then fell backward into the mattress.

Walter carried Pavia to the tiny galley kitchen off the front room. He wedged her onto the counter against the tile backsplash. He found a bottle and began to fill it with formula and tap water. He was a little clumsy at it, a little drunk he realized.

His baby was so small. The toaster, which reflected her in chrome, was nearly as big as she was. Pavia's shiny twin right here, one just for him. Just plug the bottle in, push the lever down.... Start everything over again fresh.

"Anyway," Dorothy continued from the bedroom, "Maternal wellbeing is essential to the formation of—*goddammit!*" The phone had started ringing again.

Maternal wellbeing was essential. But no one, Dorothy thought, seemed to really believe this—even though it was scientifically proven and in many other cultures around the world, Sweden or Korea for example, new mothers were given bed rest for weeks and weeks and no one expected them to do anything except relax and heal. The babies were brought to them; they (the mothers) didn't even have to go get them! Those mothers needed to rest.

Dorothy wanted to rest, too. But the baby was always there, and even though Pavia was a sweet baby and didn't cry that much, everyone else seemed to think that she, Dorothy, should always be fussing over her: feeding her or changing her or taking her for walks practically around the clock. Or cleaning things! When Pavia was three months old, Dorothy's mother, who had driven over from Miles City to stay with them, kept vacuuming and banging dishes or otherwise tidying in a way that made it clear that she, Alva, really thought that she, Dorothy, should be doing the same. And Alva fed the baby formula six times a day, at regular intervals! When Dorothy was still trying to breastfeed, and lay the foundation for a successful mother-daughter bond! When Dorothy had done quite a bit of research and felt strongly that feeding schedules were a thing of the past!

All this made Dorothy angry, which was probably bad for her milk. Did she maybe taste bitter, off? She felt that she must. And she felt anxious, worse than ever.

Luckily, Dorothy's bed was a warm raft, a place where time moved slowly enough for her to think. Off that bed, outside that bedroom, everyone was pushing her...she only had to dip her hand into the air outside of her blanket to feel the cold speed of the world.

Dorothy couldn't catch up. She didn't want to. She wanted to rest. Her bed was a warm raft, and there she stayed.

And then one afternoon when Pavia was four months old, Dorothy heard from the other room...a little gasp, a hiccup. She thought about what the sound could be, and then suddenly she knew: it was laughter, a small scrap of it. Her baby had laughed! There was Alva's voice, too, saying *That's a funny baby! Yes!*

And it was as if Dorothy had awakened from a troubled sleep, a much too-long nap—which, in fact, she really had just done—not knowing if the dim light through the curtains meant morning or afternoon. *Yes!* she heard Alva saying to her baby. She heard her baby's thin laugh again, bright as foil.

Dorothy sat up and pressed a hand to each breast. Her chest was hurting, but it wasn't her breasts; she had stopped lactating weeks ago. There wasn't anything there beneath the palms of her hands, just two fat flaps and ribs underneath them, and her heart sitting far back inside like a rock in a mailbox.

Her baby laughing, and her own mother laughing and encouraging her. As if it didn't matter what she, Dorothy, did at all. And they were happy about it! And cruel to let it show. As if Dorothy hadn't tried at all, when it was the baby, truthfully, who had refused to nurse, and fought her with kicks and tiny fists! Or stared right through her, not smiling, seeming not to see her or know her at all.

Pavia's terrible indifference, and now her laughter without her.

Her heart knocking, Dorothy got up and got dressed. She brushed her hair with long, tragic strokes, looking at herself in the mirror. With her mother and her baby in the living room, she grabbed Alva's purse from the kitchen counter and slipped out the back of the apartment. She got into her mother's car and drove to the next town, Clinton, forty miles east on the state road. She checked into the Rest Inn motel. She went to the drugstore and bought *Modern Screen*, which she had had a subscription to in high school, and then ate dinner in the motel café while she slowly leafed through the magazine. She felt the familiar chalk of its pages on her fingertips as she folded back each page....

Dorothy wondered. Did she still look like a teenager, a debutante, an ingénue? She slipped her wedding ring off her finger and put it in her purse. She smiled at the boy who filled her water glass in a way that she thought might be called *fetching*, though what did that mean, really? Dogs fetched, after all. Perhaps the idea was retrieving, as in *I have retrieved your attention, have I not?* As in, *I have regained my advantage?*

Dorothy went back to her motel room, switched on the TV, and watched it while sitting up on the bed. (She didn't want to lie down just yet. It was *My Fair Lady*.) She got a bottle of Coke from the machine in the lobby, then came back and drank it. She put all the motel towels down on the bed (Alva would approve of this), and moved the phone next to her on the mattress. She found her wedding ring in her purse and put it back on her finger. On a commercial break, she slit one of her wrists with a razor.

She felt something; not pain. A feeling of being discovered. Like a talent.

She cut her other wrist, quickly, and then, charging the call to her room, called Walter at work as the warm blood ran down her hand to her index finger to the phone's rotary dial—the dial so much like the picture wheel on a Viewmaster, in which the world's static beauty springs toward you as if in final 3-D joy.

By George, I think she's got it!

It sprang toward her.

This all happened in Supernal, Montana, a college town, home of the Runnin' Coyotes. A town in a valley, blue-green with trees and shiny with tin roofs and streetlights, a dent of culture and commerce in a state of mountains, plains, and famously Big Sky. Here my parents met, co-mingled, married, and stayed. They had my sister (see above). Here my father finished school with a degree in General Studies and a promotion to Assistant Manager of Produce at Buttrey's Market. In the black early morning, he met the trucks at the loading dock, and helped carry in the boxes. The greasy marks on the dock were the fruits and vegetables that had fallen out of the boxes and been stepped on over the years; there was a section of concrete near the edge that looked like that painting, *Starry Night*, only the opposite, the swirls dark as drains.

During those years at the market, was Walter well-groomed and reliable? Did he greet customers with a smile and an inquiry (*Have you noticed that our sweet corn is in?*)? Did he perform key tasks and manage other duties as assigned? For example, did he devise clever signage (*How's them apples? 40 cents a pound!*)? Was he careful to rotate the heads of lettuce so that the fresher ones were in the back, and did he tear off the browning leaves?

Walter did these things only occasionally and not well. He did enjoy aiming the carrots all in one direction, however. He made a hellfire of raining orange arrows.

But did he, as his widower father often suggested to him in those early years, make the most of this opportunity within the Buttrey's Company, striving to work his way up, joining the Rotary Club or the Masons so as to make potentially useful business connections? Was his handshake firm? Did he have the manager and his wife to his apartment for dinner occasionally? Or did he perhaps think that a psychiatric institution—as they were far more humane than they used to be, not like *The Snake Pit* or similar, staffed by trained doctors and achieving miraculous results in hundreds of people every single day—might not be a suitable place for Dorothy, for a while?

Walter considered these and others of his father's suggestions, but his mind would never stay on them. He couldn't do them. For one thing, he didn't want to give his father the satisfaction. For another, his father's voice on the phone reminded him powerfully that he was already forgetting the sound of his mother's voice. The way his mother said his name—*Wal-ter*—the first syllable with a falling note as if her mouth was also trying to smile while she said his name. Most of all, he just couldn't think of self-improvement. Standing in his stained apron, piling potatoes and turnips and parsnips, he couldn't focus on these bright and reasonable suggestions. He felt too dark, buried.

Every day he felt himself reaching deeper downward—on purpose, he had to admit, because some part of him must want this blind and twisting kind of striving—a human tuber.

By this time, Alva had moved in with them permanently. At the grocery store one day, Walter overheard her explaining to the checkout girl that Dorothy had Continuing Poor Health and needed a Great Deal of Rest; she (Alva) felt fortunate to be able to help.

Fortunate. Fortunate? Walter turned the word over in his mind the way people he observed in the produce section—housewives—looked for soft spots on melons. Fortunate was... what? It was Pavia, he decided. His baby girl, her fat hands reaching out for him when he came home. Dorothy had chosen her name; it was the name of a university in Italy where the editor of Dorothy's anthropology textbook had once been a Distinguished Fellow. "The name," Dorothy had said while she was pregnant and happy, "is beautiful, unusual, and not too difficult." Walter thought about this now. Pavia really *was* all of these things—beautiful, unusual, not too difficult—and in this, at least, he was fortunate. And fortunately and unfortunately, there was Alva. He tried to think of her as a piece of domestic machinery—a labor-saving appliance, like a vacuum cleaner—that kept his baby fed and clean, and it was their job (his and Dorothy's) to stay out of the way. They ought to be able to do that, to be appreciative. But unfortunately, he was too tired.

Then one day, as in every story, something happened. Walter, walking home from work in the early morning, went to put his can of Rainier beer in a trash outside the library. He happened to look up at the newly lit windows and the tall letters above the doorway.

Supernal Public Library.

He stood there. He became aware that *he* was part of the public—he could dimly hear his father saying, "you have responsibilities now"—and that *he* could go in. He could go in and not go home to the apartment. For a while. And it would be all right. You can't fault someone for spending too much time at the library, after all. It's a citizen's duty to be informed. He could check out *Popular Science*, for example. *Life. Look.*

So he went in that morning, and almost every morning thereafter. Judith Callahan, head librarian with a brunette wig styled in a crisp, shoulder-length flip, offered him a part-time position shelving books. He took it as a second job. Eventually, he was offered a full-time job in Reference, and he quit Buttrey's and accepted it.

"That's not a career," his father told him on the phone. "Sales! Sales has income potential."

"Boys working at libraries," his mother-in-law said the same night, grimacing a little as she pressed the steam button on the iron. "What do you wear to work?"

Dorothy liked the idea, however. "It's the life of the mind," she said. She was sitting on the couch, watching Pavia toddle toward her across the living room. Dorothy looked like Pavia, Walter thought then, or the other way around—their dark hair and softness. Their sweetness.

"The coffee table!" Alva suddenly growled. "Watch the baby!" With surprising speed she lurched on phlebitic legs around the ironing board to intercept Pavia.

"Your insurance likely won't be as good now," she grunted, catching Pavia under the arms.

For some reason at this moment Walter looked at Dorothy. She was looking back at him. "Surrounded by books and great ideas," she said softly to him, and she smiled at her husband as her baby was dragged, whimpering, backward away from her across the carpet.

One year later, I was born.

Born unto a librarian, I am named for the goddess of sight, a yogic cosmologist, the long-lost daughter of Cleopatra and Caesar, a low-rent mistress of Harold Lloyd. My godmother is Judith Callahan, secretly bald chief librarian. I was born a Scorpio, in the year of the rooster, and with a 28% increased risk of a mood disorder, likely with other mental health comorbidities. I suffer from myopia and have required corrective lenses since age five. Yet all my life, I considered myself lucky—*fortunate*—for I was born the sister of Pavia.

Neither of us, we two daughters of Walter and Dorothy, was born cute. We are not petite, we have not the blonde hair and wide, winning smiles, nor yet the pert, lordotic butt-tilt so much favored in our hometown of Supernal. Still, Pavia has always been beautiful. Long limbed, tallish, she has hazel eyes and dark brown hair like I do—yet unlike me, she doesn't ruin the effect by talking too much or moving her face in odd ways. As far as I can tell, no one has ever told her to calm down, get over it, or go away. Instead, people are always trying to get her attention. When, in sixth grade, a boy scratched her name in his forearm with a ballpoint pen, she glanced at it only long enough to correct his spelling.

"And on the other arm?" she said, smoothing her smooth hair behind her ear, "You've got, 'I love Satin.' You mean Satan, right? S-A-T-A-N?"

The boy stared at her. Inside his slightly open mouth, his tongue pulsed once as he swallowed. He loved her. Everyone does.

Which was difficult to understand, as were most things about our Pavia. She defied all of the expectations established by the child development book Dorothy consulted from time to time—a lime-green paperback with a black and white photo of three children grimly stacking blocks. For example, according to the author Dr. Guesten, Pavia, being an ectomorph like her father, could be expected to be neurotic, hypersensitive, prone to concealment and dependency. She was none of these things. Doctor Guesten also predicted many unsettling behavioral phases, phases in which the maternal influence would be particularly potent, the most marked of which would occur at ages eighteen months, three years, and five years.

Yet at eighteen months, Pavia belonged entirely to her grandmother Alva. It was Alva who fed her and dressed her. It was Alva who moved with her through the apartment, shushing and sweeping. She sometimes ruffled Pavia's hair before smoothing it down.

So did Dorothy, sometimes.

At age three—Dr. Guesten's second behavioral milestone—Pavia had a new baby sister (me). On the advice of chapter four, Dorothy encouraged Pavia to acknowledge sibling rivalry. She tried to promote constructive ways that Pavia's inferred rage could be healthily exercised—for example, through Regression Outlets. Yet when Dorothy spoke baby-talk to Pavia, Pavia ignored her. When Dorothy invited her to nurse at her breast alongside her baby sister, Pavia ran to hide in the hall closet. Clearly Pavia wanted neither regression nor outlet.

However, Pavia did display some of the hallmark characteristics of this fascinating age of three years; she was indeed defiant and intractable, for example. But this could have been because Dorothy got sick again soon after the baby sister was born, which compelled Dorothy once again to stay in bed as after Pavia's birth. Or, it could have been because Alva suddenly died of a heart attack. She had been lifting a bag of Johnny Kat in the garage, intending to sprinkle the cat litter on the front steps as extra traction in the ice. Alva was still holding the bag in her arms when Walter found her, a gray Pietà, next to her Plymouth.

And at five years old—the last of the developmental moments drawn with such detail, like studies for a sculpture in Dr. G's landmark tome—Pavia was not clingy and withdrawn. She was, her kindergarten teacher Mrs. Cullum said, unusually self-possessed. Well regulated. Independent. Self-starting. Dorothy had to agree: in the mornings, Pavia ate and got dressed by herself, fixed her hair herself (she had to get the aerodynamics exactly right, the pigtails angled downward and oriented to the back as if to suggest at a glance that *she was going places*), walked to school by herself. At the end of the day, she made her way home and unaided found *Gilligan's Island* reruns on the television.

And at this time of the day, her baby sister Thea, a typically noisy and vigorous mesomorph, would crawl across the shag carpeting to her side and put her heavy head in Pavia's lap. Sometimes, Pavia would ruffle her hair.

Inside the TV, on that distant island, Ginger Grant pined for her lost audience. Mary Ann missed home cooking. Together the two girls Ginger and Mary Ann put on shows and baked coconut cream pies, making the best of things. My sister and I saw every episode from 18 inches away, the sound turned up very high because Dorothy—lying on her bed in the back bedroom—wanted to know where we were at all times. The sound of the laugh track could reach her ears this way, and reassure her.

Later in life, if I become deaf, that is why.

5. IT'S BETTER BEFORE YOU KNOW WHAT IT IS

When the dark-eyed hairstylist—looking past you in the mirror at herself—draws her comb slowly across your scalp.

When the plug in the bathtub is taken out and the water—ever colder, dense as mercury in a thermometer—pulls on your skin as it drains.

Once when the infant you're holding looks up at you and you empty through your own eyes. He reaches, you open your mouth, you feel his sharp fingers on your tongue. They are salt and metal, like your own tears, like wanting something.

6. YOUR CHILD IS AN ARROW

With General at her side, Pavia led me up the steps to her townhouse and unlocked the door.

"Two locks?" I said. "A deadbolt?"

"Big city," Pavia said. We entered a tall, narrow hall and pushed our way forward, scraping the walls with my suitcase and duffle bags. "And you'll also notice very little sign of Jack."

"He's gone already?" I felt deflated, irritated. I'd come all this way while developing a bad headache, and the trouble was already over? The muscles in the back of my neck—the trapezius, the splenius capitis—felt tight, plucked, old-timey and banjo-annoying.

We had entered a large kitchen. The cabinets were black, the floor was wood, the gleaming refrigerator was bare of photos, schedules, or post-its with handwritten scrawls of positive self-talk—I CAN OWN MY FEELINGS, for example—and the sink had no dishes in it. The counters were bare except for an electric mixer with a bowl, a food processor, and a coffee machine, which I examined closely.

"Wow," I remarked. "You have an expresso machine?"

"*Esp*resso. Employee recognition gift." Pavia put my bags on the floor next to General's huge stainless steel water bowl and sat down at a wooden table. She reached for a bag of mini rice cakes and glanced around the room. "You're just used to mom's kitchen, which is ugly. And dirty. And suburban." She still had her coat on. "Want to make some coffee for us?"

She talked me through the process of making an espresso, and thus I learned the essential skill of my generation. I also learned, as we talked about Jack's absence, the essential and unconvincing story, which was:

She thought she loved him, but maybe she didn't after all. Maybe she just needed something to do, or someone to (pretend to) love. (Maybe, admittedly, he did, too.) Maybe she discovered that he was not the person she thought he was—or maybe it was her fault. Maybe she had changed? And it was sad but probably—most likely, almost surely—their breakup was all for the best in the long run.

My sister finished talking and looked at me in a way that I recognized—with a little stab of fear—as hope-filled.

"What did the asshole do?" I asked.

"Nothing." Pavia looked away, turning to watch General slop water into his mouth, his tongue folding and unfolding like an envelope flap as it went in and out of his enormous head. She still had her hand in the rice-cake bag. She looked exhausted.

"What did the asshole do?" The espresso machine hissed reinforcingly behind me.

Pavia frowned, shook her head no. "He's not an asshole, Thea." She put a rice cake in her mouth and chewed down and up quickly, suddenly as alert and skittish-seeming as a parking lot sparrow. "He got a promotion. He started golfing. He wears knit shirts." She took a deep breath in and held it. "He was very happy."

Pavia said "happy" and dropped her dark head down into the bend of her elbow on the table. Her rice-cake hand remained aloft in a shape reminiscent of the big city's controversial airport sculpture, *Flight of Progress*.

My sister cried—not loudly, but not softly, either. I waited uncertainly. I found some ibuprofen in her cabinet and swallowed it and came back to the table and sat down again, still waiting, now stifling a weird giddiness. Seeing Pavia like this—emotionally labile and not particularly well-groomed—filled me with frightened, sisterly gratitude.

In the short-term, as she wept, I needed to figure out what I ought to say. Truthfully, although we had shared a bedroom for fifteen years and logged countless hours side by side in front of the television, we had never talked much to each other. I had acquired the impression that in general, Pavia believed that one's feelings were beside the point. Yet there she was with her head on the table, manifesting feeling, seeming to want me to say something.

I cleared my throat and began to sing quietly. "He's just a poor boy!" I leaned close to her ear, "From a poor family!"

I grabbed her salty claw and shook it; salt sifted down like dandruff. I began the song again, shaking her arm hard with each beat: "He's-just-a-poor-boy, from-a-poor fam-i-ly…!"

"Scaramouche," Pavia sniffled, her voice both muffled and magnified by the table mere inches from her face. "Scaramouche." She lifted her head and wiped her reddened face with the back of her clean hand.

I breathed a note of relief and unclutched my sister then. I stood up, took off my coat, poured us each some coffee. I thought to myself, if Jack's actually gone, and they have an espresso machine and Pavia is hurting, maybe I should stay a while. Perhaps the big city is for me. My headache was lifting already.

"And?" I asked Pavia after a few re-calming minutes had

passed. "Jack was happy, you say?"

"Happy, yeah. And when he left, I got General. For some reason I was really wanting a dog. And you know, Great Danes only live three or four years." She, too, had brightened considerably and rapidly.

"And what about your job?" Pavia and Jack worked at the same software company. Jack was sales, Pavia was leadership training.

"Fine. Same. I got a promotion, too." Now Pavia reached down for General, who licked her salty hand noisily. "I've got to get him neutered. Can you believe he's still just a puppy?" She looked up at me and then glanced at the clock on the stove. "Hey, I've got to walk him in the park before dinner. Come with me?"

"Well, yeah, sure. But Pavia," I said as she stood up and scraped her chair backward. "Seriously. Why is Jack gone?"

She pulled her hair up behind her head, twisted an elastic around it. "I asked him to leave. And he was heartbroken."

I silently considered that: Jack's heart like a dessert plate dropped on the ground.

"*Heartbroken*. His exact phrase," my sister said over her shoulder. I followed her and her enviable ponytail out of the kitchen and back down the hall. She leaned down to pick up General's leash by the front door.

"And I looked around at all this"—she gestured vaguely toward the coat rack, up to the hallway light fixture—"and I just don't want to bring a child into this world." General shoved his way past her out the door.

"All this what?" I demanded, but she was already tripping down the front steps looking like a model in an autumn clothing catalog—all woolens and outdoor high jinks—and in her cheeks as she turned back to look at me, a sudden healthy high color.

So that was it: a tiny lightbulb turned on inside, one watt of new life, a fetus.

"Into all this *what*?" I shouted after her again.

In the next several days we didn't talk about whether Pavia would have an abortion. My sister hinted that the fetus might, like Jack, go away with the right kind of discouragement on her part. She was eight weeks along. She was still running every day, wearing tight pants, using toxic cleaning products. She was still drinking coffee and cocktails. If she had morning sickness, she wasn't admitting it.

"It's a tradition for people in our family to just drop dead one day," she told me, citing Grandma Alva and Grandma Claudia.

I knew what she was thinking. "What if it's just the females, though? This baby could be a boy. Plus, think about mom." We both knew implicitly: Dorothy would be the lingering type. She would live forever.

Pavia shrugged. There was still plenty of time for something to happen. Every trip to the bathroom, Pavia confirmed, included a probing, exploratory wipe for signs of a mishap.

But there was nothing like that. Instead, over the next weeks and then months in the big city, all developments quietly developed.

Jack called a lot, but seemed to be titrating downward. Pavia bought a cordless phone so she could move around the house while she listened to him. Cradling the receiver between her shoulder and chin gave her the awkward bent head of an Orthodox Madonna while she folded laundry, watered the houseplants, did sit-ups. She listened to her husband with a Coptic inscrutability, disagreeing gently from time to time.

Meanwhile, the fetus did this, that, and the other. It was the size of a pinhead, a polyp, a Pez. I inferred all this, of course, based on the library books I had checked out. Pavia wasn't reading them and hadn't gotten around to seeing a doctor.

Similarly, I hadn't gotten around to returning home to Supernal. I signed up with a temp agency, and had a series of non-taxing receptionist positions. I became aware of the possibility—indeed the necessity—of having nicer shoes, and I bought several pairs which I lined up under the bed in the small guest room Pavia had turned over to me. Most significantly, I went with Pavia to rock shows at the club around the corner from her townhouse, The Arrow. The consequence was a series of thrilling one-night stands with boys who worked in coffee shops, bookstores, and guitar shops. I was twenty-four, and the only boyfriend I had ever had was Adam, and I was shocked to find out that in the right town—a bigger city—even a girl with glasses and slightly hairy forearms could garner male attention. Also that, contrary to everything my high school health teacher had told me, promiscuity did not lead to disease, depression, and unplanned pregnancy. Rather, it resulted in feelings of ease, power, and possibility. I mean, of course, that I felt *hot*, and grateful for it.

Somewhere along in here, one night in early fall, I called up Dorothy and filled her in on the nature of the dilemma I'd been sent to address: Pavia was pregnant and getting a divorce. I told her that I was going to stay there, in the big city. To provide support.

Pavia and I were watching TV on the couch when I called; to muffle the sound, I put my hand over the receiver after I spoke and waited for my mother's reaction.

In fact, Dorothy felt a great energy around this news. A Great Energy! Then she handed the phone over to someone she introduced as Joseph and made me tell him the same news.

"Right on," said Joseph, "Peace." He then hung up on me, and I turned to Pavia.

"He's her new friend," she told me, flipping through the TV channels. "She's in a mood. She's been calling me at work, asking for money."

I felt my teeth clench together. According to Dorothy, my jaw is my primary stress storage area. "Are you sending her money then?"

Still staring at the screen, Pavia pulled her legs off the floor to sit cross-legged on the couch. "Yeah. Sure. So?"

I began working my jaw like that martial little Nutcracker, up and down, up and down, trying to loosen it up.

I was used to Dorothy being sad. In my mind, she still belonged in the damp-smelling back bedroom where she slept most of the day, most of the years of our childhood. When Pavia and I were growing up, Dorothy's rare forays into the rest of the house had seemed benign. Pope-like in a flannel housecoat, she emerged each morning before school to wave her hand weakly over our cereal bowls and read aloud the day's affirmation from her flip calendar. *I am guided into my true place. I trust the universe to provide abundantly for me now. I am a perfect jewel of wholeness.* But in the last few years, starting before Pavia's wedding, things had begun to change. Sometimes Dorothy was up, full of energy. "I feel happy," she would tell me, crediting Saturn's perigee or an herbal infusion. "And you know what? I deserve it."

I agreed with her, actually, so I decided I approved of Pavia sending her money. We can handle this episode, I thought, so long as Pavia keeps being responsible. Clenching and unclenching my jaw while Pavia smiled indulgently at the television, I reached for the book she'd left on the table by the couch. I opened it to the middle.

Change is threat, wrote the famed management consultant truthfully.

If Dorothy was going to be happy (not to mention financially irresponsible), if I was going to have a social (sex) life and wear cute shoes and vintage dresses, then Pavia—even through her marital issues and unplanned pregnancy—was going to have to continue to hold things together.

A three-legged stool, warned the consultant, *is not the most stable structure.*

One Saturday morning when Pavia was at the grocery store and I was watching Power Rangers on the couch, Jack knocked at the door, then let himself in with his house key. He wanted to pick up some of his stuff.

As my family of origin is not the type to reunite routinely, I hadn't seen Jack since his wedding seven years earlier. He still had all his pale hair—a doll's head of hair, each fat strand washable and alert-looking—but he looked older. It was mostly an effect of the uncertain expression on his pink face; nevertheless I also noted that nothing makes a person look more vulnerable than a too-small sweatshirt, relic of one's freshman year, bunching under one's armpits, the words *Montana Trout!* above a C-shaped fish straining for the fly.

I explained to Jack what Pavia was doing (shopping) and what I was suffering from (hangover).

"Can I get you some orange juice?" he asked gently. "Turn up the heat? I've had a few morning-afters myself." I nodded pathetically. I knew he'd prefer to pity me, rather than the other way around; after all, if I had recently been rejected by my spouse I'd probably want to adopt a neglected animal, one missing a limb or an eye. I accepted a glass of juice and a blanket, and Jack went upstairs to pack.

Pavia came home just as Jack was carrying two suitcases down the stairs.

"Hey," my sister said quickly, frowning, then smiling.

General stood in front of her with his tail whipping the wall, his snout burrowing deep into her crotch—working through it like a French pig hunting truffles.

"Cute trick," Jack said, looking down at General. "Got your period?" He started down the stairs again. His suitcases and her plastic grocery bags jostled against each other as he eased his way past his wife in the entryway.

"Now that I'm single, maybe I should get a dog like that," Jack said, turning around at the open door to look at Pavia. He smiled like it hurt—as if his jaw, too, stored excess psychic tension. "I could take that dog to the bars with me, and he'd be able to tell me who I shouldn't bother pursuing that night."

Pavia shook her hair out of her eyes, waited. "Jack," she said. Her voice was low and excruciatingly patient. "I don't have my period. I'm pregnant."

Jack stared back at her. He took a deep breath; the trout on his shirt magnified momentarily, like something lifted from the water and then put back. From my vantage point on the couch, I felt a wave of new nausea. I buried my head in the cushion and breathed through my mouth.

"Mine?" I heard Jack say.

Hee-ahh! screamed the Power Rangers from inside their shining helmets, inside the TV.

Pavia said something. "Later," she said more loudly after a moment, and I heard the front door shut, heard her stomp past me down the hall toward the kitchen.

Carefully, I raised my head then and got to my feet. I followed my sister into the kitchen.

"Hey," I said. Pavia ignored me and began to put away the groceries. "Do you remember what Mom always told us about your baptism?"

"Yeah." Reaching to put soup into the cupboard, Pavia's

coat swept open. Her stomach was round under her sweater; why hadn't I noticed this before?

"She wanted to read Kahlil Gibran but the minister said no because Gibran wasn't a Christian. That made her so mad she never went to church again. I wasn't even baptized."

Pavia wadded up a plastic bag and threw it toward the trashcan, missed. "I think he was some kind of Christian, actually."

"The quote was, 'Your children are not yours, they are like arrows, you are just the bow. Let them fly freely.'"

"She had that quote taped to the fridge, too."

"But Dorothy ignored us," I said. My face felt suddenly hot. "She did nothing for us."

"She didn't get in our way."

"She was always too tired to do anything. Everything was too much trouble."

"She was always supportive."

"She was fucking lame." A little arrow of bile rose up in my throat. I went to stand by the sink.

Pavia closed a cabinet door and turned to look at me.

"So what though?" She used the same voice she had used with Jack, a maternal tone carrying out over a vast distance like an echo of the original Eve, the blithe, guilty one. "You know? So, what?"

"So...so is that Jack's? Jack's baby?" I felt my face twist up in ugly pre-cry shapes, my glasses rising askew across the bridge of my nose.

"Jesus, Thea. What's wrong with you?"

"Pavia," I said, "It needs to be somebody's."

Pavia leaned back on the refrigerator, lifting her chin and slowly rolling the curve of her skull across the freezer door. "It's not like I had sex with anyone else." She gave a little snort. "You've seen the way I live. I'm completely celibate these days."

"So what happens then? Is it—?" I started again, "Are you having it?"

Her fingers drummed the refrigerator door. "I don't know. I guess," my sister said. "I guess this creature's here to stay." She looked down at her torso with an expression of confused expectation, like someone who had just been served the wrong entrée at a restaurant. She put her hand—ringless, the left—on her stomach, wiped it once on her sweater, then looked at me. "I'll have the baby most of the time. Jack travels too much. And...I don't know. He might not really be on board with this pregnancy. He, um, he didn't know until today."

"Clearly."

With a kind of wild impersonality, she smiled and looked away. Her hair had gotten longer and darker, shiny as a pelt.

"I don't go anywhere either," I said then, which wasn't true but could become true, if she wanted. "I can help with the baby. I'm underemployed."

"Underemployed? What do you mean; you need money?"

"It just means my jobs are boring."

I watched Pavia's fingers crawl across the ribbing of her sweater at her waistline. She pressed her fingers on her enlarging torso, thinking about me.

"I can change that, I bet," she said, poking in hard.

7. HUMILIATION AS A NEAR RHYME

On the oldies station someday—the oldies podcast—you'll eventually hear about the fifty ways to leave your lover. They rhyme: *Hop on the bus, Gus. Make a new plan, Stan. Slip out the back, Jack.*

In life, of course, they don't rhyme. They are unmusical, anti-musical, like the sound of a needle skipping across the record, which for you will also be just another artifact, another oldie. Imagine it therefore as the sound of something being unzipped. Or ripped.

In the big city that fall, I had a Québécois boyfriend for ten days. With him, I practiced my high school French and my library-researched sex moves, those that were Gallic-seeming, rough, slightly unhygienic. And at my prompting one night, he—let's call him Gilles—confessed his private penseés, namely his désir for ultra fun.

Ultra fun? Fun? For a moment, I felt silly, frilly, rhyme-y. Moi?

"Autre femme! Another woman!" Gilles finally hissed between his beautiful, if smoke-stained, teeth. "I want to be with her, not you!"

Not me. *Pas moi.* See? That's the one that rhymes.

8. VENITE ADOREMUS

The ex-boyfriend to whom I have earlier referred had a grandfather who owned a cabin on Amsterdam Lake, three hours from Supernal. We—Adam and I—used to go there sometimes for weekends. It was an ideal place for completing term papers, smoking cigarettes, setting off the illegal firecrackers we bought on the Indian reservation. It was where we ate hallucinogenic mushrooms for the first time and, after the melting nausea, felt miraculously whole and perfect. And it was on the drive to Amsterdam Lake that I began to put Adam's mother's lumbar-supporting travel pillow inside my shirt. Whenever we stopped for gas, I would tuck the pillow deep into my waistband in the front, and I would rise from the passenger side slowly, majestically, heavy with ersatz child.

Yes, I rested my hand—perhaps unconsciously—atop my swelling womb as I browsed the aisles of the truck stop stores of state road 83.

Yes, I was serene. I gazed benignly at the Funyons arrayed on the metal rack as if for my express pleasure.

Yes, I bore the hardships of pregnancy uncomplainingly.

While Adam paid for the gas I stood beside him, and only the arching of my lower back betrayed my discomfort.

Yes, I'm due in April. Yes, it's our first. Yes, we're very excited. I answered queries shyly.

Adam would shove his wallet into his back pocket and grimly thank the clerk. He would push his way out of the store, letting the glass door swing back on me.

"Come *on*." Driving away, I'd be frustrated, amused—an awkward combination that I value now as a coping response. "People love young couples. It gives them an orgasm just to see us. It's all Brother Sun and Sister Moon—all afternoon delight."

But Adam claimed to have a personal policy against lying. I still can picture the blotches on the sides of his pale neck as he said this. I assumed this was his tell, the way he unconsciously signaled a deception.

Because I lie like a rug, of course. I always have. I lied, for example, about being on birth control for all the years Adam and I were together. I had a personal policy about it, a *position*, namely that it was my business. Mine. *What happens in Vegas, stays in Vegas*: you stick an unprotected penis in a vaginal canal and it, my friend, is on its own. I could understand why Pavia hadn't told Jack right away about her pregnancy.

In any case, during all that time with Adam, I never got pregnant. Later, in the big city, despite an initial bolus of casual sex, same thing: no dice. I started to imagine my uterus like an airport windsock—thin-walled, half-slack, the wind blowing through and leaving nothing behind except a general indication: *they went thataway, southeast.*

Just as she'd promised, Pavia helped me get a full-time job. The job was working for her boss's wife, Charmaine, copyediting for QmedCare. "Do you know the difference between 'that' and 'which'?" Charmaine asked me in my interview. I said I did.

QmedCare is America's number one resource for high quality, regulatorily compliant medical education materials. At QMedCare we wrote for nurses: "A patient fall is an unplanned descent to the floor, with or without injury to the patient." Here, my task would be to double-check the definition in my bound copy of the regulations. (Correct.)

We wrote for physicians. Here my priority needed to be the scrupulous enforcement of the passive voice: "In the absence of key indicators, clinical judgment should be applied in the determination of disease presence."

We wrote for patients: "Even with urinary incontinence, you can still lead a full life." In this case, I would elect to change "full" to "active."

I liked this job. In Supernal, I could never have earned real money correcting "their" and "there" or replacing "doctor" with "healthcare provider." It was a relief after waitressing, my only non-temp job since college graduation, at which—despite sincere and sustained efforts—I was hypocompetent. Now that I had a real job at QmedCare, I could finally admit to myself how much I had hated my restaurant day-shift full of brisk small talk and the need to carry three plates at a time. I hated eye contact via food-spattered glasses; I had had real difficulty reciting the daily specials with a straight face. And oh, the forgotten condiments, the poorly timed coffee refills! Verily I was glad to get away from all that, the feeling that I was disappointing someone every day.

Life in the big city was far easier than life in a small college town, I was finding. Why do people tell you otherwise?

Pavia's pregnancy entered the second trimester. The fetus was probably the size of a joy buzzer. Probably, it had eyes and eyebrows.

After a couple of weeks of me researching at work and then describing to Pavia the varieties of genetic slip-up the fetus might be affected by—various eponymous syndromes, the results of chromosomes snapping off or misaligning on the helix like the teeth of a cheap plastic zipper—Pavia made the appointment with an obstetrician near our townhouse, downtown.

"Physical exam, bloodwork, ultrasound—the works," she said. "So no more about the fluid-filled heads, all right?"

As I've mentioned, my sister had always had the calmness characteristic of certain beautiful people. This population is characterized by the unfurrowed brow, the unhurried gait, the modulated and pleasant tone of voice. As a group, they probably sleep well. They are not nail biters; they do not pick their scabs. Their shirts maintain all original buttons. They make excellent corporate trainers, supermodels, and (I'm thinking) ambassadors and ambassadors' wives. As sisters, they are reliable if inscrutable.

So, as promised, Pavia arranged to take the afternoon off to go to the doctor's. I took the whole day off for the occasion, and met her at noon as she stepped off the commuter train. It was ten days before Christmas, cold. A few dry flakes of snow drifted sideways among the office buildings in a confused, retarded way. We walked with our coats pulled tight around us.

"Exciting, right? You're going to see the baby and all?" I asked.

"Hmm." Pavia said.

With my head tucked down I felt the wind on the side part on top of my head. Our store-window reflections hurried next to us, mine a half step behind Pavia's and revealing the slightly twisting and cramped gait of a race walker.

"Nervous?" I asked.

Pavia ducked into a doorway and I followed. We crossed the

lobby and went into an open elevator, Pavia unwinding her scarf and holding the door open for me with one expensive boot. I got in and she punched the button for the eleventh floor.

The OB's office waiting room was painted in the greens and lavenders favored by the aromatherapy industry. Framed children's drawings had been mounted above every third chair along the edges of the room. A half-dozen women of child-bearing age—randomized, controlled—looked up at us as we came in, reviewed our shoes and outfits, then went back to their magazines.

While Pavia checked in, I picked up the magazine on the table next to me. On the cover, a new mom, looking jazzed, pressed her nose into her newborn's stunned and wizened face. And when my sister rejoined me—sitting down heavily next to me, minus a clipboard of new-patient papers—I had to ask, "You've been here before, haven't you?"

I said it in the arch way of female detectives on TV, all of them single and difficult to amuse.

"Last spring," Pavia admitted. She took the magazine lying on my lap and ran her hand over the cover. "This mom looks like she's gonna eat him, poor kid," she observed. After a moment she glanced at me sideways. "So yeah. I was here last spring. I was pregnant, and then I wasn't." She began flipping the pages of the magazine. "Miscarriage."

"You were still with Jack?"

Pavia nodded.

"I can't imagine him sitting in this waiting room, for some reason."

"Me neither," Pavia said. "But he was." Paging past the magazine's beaming moms and infants, my sister's unconscious copycat smile was vulgar even to me. "He really, really wanted that one."

She looked up at me then, her borrowed smile still hanging

on her features. "Hah hah hah," she laughed—ironically, I'll allow—but I was disconcerted all the same. More and more, I thought with a slow and lacerating dismay, Pavia was becoming like a person going through a divorce or worse.

"Let's not go home," I said as we came out of the building an hour later. "Let's walk and shop and drink coffee."

"All right," Pavia surprised me by saying. "Where to?"

We went to the neighborhood around the world famous university, where the narrow streets teemed with young people lit from within by their own bright futures. They had such gleaming faces and knowing laughter, such seeming ease—personal and interpersonal—that I felt the climate shifting as we walked among them, their self-regard moisturizing the air, reducing the appearance of fine lines and improving the clarity and evenness of their already-fine complexions. It was an atmosphere that Pavia, at least, should have felt comfortable in. I followed her as she slid her way into a café and stood at the counter waiting to order.

"Two things to tell you," I said to Pavia. "First: mom. She called yesterday and said she's coming for Christmas."

"I know. She's been threatening for a while. They're driving, if you can believe it."

"Who's 'they'?"

"She's with that guy. Joseph."

I stomped my feet to dislodge imaginary snow. "Maybe she still won't make it. Maybe she'll get distracted."

"Maybe."

We ordered coffee and pastries and carried them to one of the little metal tables near the window. Outside, a small group of young men sang "Rudolph the Red-Nosed Reindeer" in Latin.

"Is it possible to sing in one of these a capella groups without that... *expression* on your face?" I asked.

Pavia shrugged. Elbow to elbow at the table, we watched the young men keening with their hands in their long bankers' coats, mugging and harmonizing. We plunged our pastries in our coffee cups in between bites and watched the singers start the song again. Despite myself I began to hum along.

Reno erat Rudolphus
Nosum rubum habebat
Si quando hunc videbas
Hunc candere tu dicas

"What's the second thing?" Pavia asked at last. "That second thing to tell me?"

"Oh," I said. "Maybe it's nothing. But still. I met a boy."

I told her about Eli, the plant guy in my building at work. Twice a week down the carpeted hallways of our office he pulled a small wagon that held a large plastic water container with a coiled spray hose coming out of the top. Eli was thin and tall and had brown eyes and messy brown hair; he wore a carpenter's belt with various clippers and soil pokers. He often wore a faded Cramps t-shirt and worn Toughskins. I told Pavia: Along with the guys who scaled the outside of the building to clean the windows, along with the mud-spattered bicycle messengers, he was my type as I was beginning to understand it.

"What? Skinny? Working in appliance-requiring non-skilled labor?" Pavia raised one of her perfect, boomerang-shaped eyebrows. "Maybe it's just that there are hardly any men in your office. How do you feel about the UPS guy?"

"I don't like those shorts. No. Anyway, our UPS guy whistles."

"So do you."

"I don't whistle *while I work*."

Pavia nodded, took another bite of her pastry. She looked at me as she chewed. She nudged me with her foot under the table, waiting for me to go on. And suddenly, as if I were an accelerator pedal, I felt a surge of primitive, desperate affection for my sister. Like how Jack, having won her attention and approval for a moment, would probably always want it back.

Eli, I told Pavia, was quiet, but he had a nice laugh. He wanted to be a photographer; he *was* a photographer. He did take pictures. We had had coffee twice after work.

"How did you manage that?"

"It happened like this," I said, and I began the story in the traditional way, with the setting:

I worked in a cubicle, 10 feet by 4 feet, the walls of which were gray polyblend fabric over plastic planks. The back wall was covered—as if by tiny drill team members or miniature girl Communists—with little red and white flags. These flags were the fortunes from every cookie I'd received for every lunch since I started at QMedCare and began to frequent the Chinese takeout on the first floor of our building. One-fourth of these fortunes read, *You are wise among men.* Another several warned, *Listen not to futile words of vain tongue.* One day, I was sitting in front of my computer staring at my favorite flag—the enigmatic *We are happy together*—when I realized I was listening.

I knew the sound that the rubber wheels of Eli's cart made on our no-pile commercial carpet. I could recognize the sound of him squirting the plants along the corridor, the sound of his voice, softly saying *Fuck*, when his cart banged into our department's printer table. I was hearing these sounds now, and without thinking about it, I stood up. My wheeled chair rolled away from the backs of my knees like an ellipsis....

"What is this plant called?" I blurted as Eli rounded the corner near my cube. In front of me, I was holding the dusty spider plant that had been sitting on top of my bookshelf since I arrived at QMedCare.

Eli's untidy eyebrows went up, down, together. "Well," he said at last, pointing his spray nozzle at the pot, "That's a jacaranda."

"What about that one?" I asked, pointing behind him at a yellowing ivy.

"Alpine buttercup."

"And that?"

"Pavlovian thistle."

"Ah," I said, and we stood there facing each other for a moment, grinning. Then Eli said, "Do you drink coffee?"

And so it came to pass that we went to coffee that day, a Tuesday, and again on Thursday. The second time, as we were walking back toward the elevator bank on the first floor of the building, Eli nudged me gently into one of the giant potted palm trees meant to enliven the building's barren corporate atrium. "Outta the way, ma'am," he drawled. I staggered happily toward the elevator. In super slow motion, he elbowed me across the chest to reach the up button first.

I looked at the lit button, aware of Eli's rate of respiration. When the elevator door opened, I waited for him to step inside ahead of me. "Get in there, punk," I breathed.

And then the door closed. It got quiet. I saw my face reflected in the control panel; I was smiling too widely—almost rectangularily—and my eyes were wide behind my glasses, manic with bare hope. *Oh no*, I thought, and I braced myself. And then Eli reached out. He grabbed my waist and pulled me in, and the elevator got sucked up the shaft as we went down together, weak-kneed, like two soft metals to an alloy.

"And he pulled me in," I said to Pavia sitting across from me at the wobbly metal table.

She folded her arms on the table and looked at me. She exhaled audibly through her nostrils, making the pastry flakes in her neck scarf tremble.

"Hormones," my sister said suddenly, taking in a little gulp of air. And she pressed a balled-up napkin to the corners of her shining eyes.

At the obstetrician's office, earlier that day, the technician had led us down the hall. She brought us into a small room with a low cushioned table and told Pavia to climb up and slide her pants down. Then the tech—young and fair-haired with a border of peach-colored makeup visible in front of her ears—sat down on a wheeled stool and swiveled to face the ultrasound screen.

"First baby?" she sang out to us, fiddling with the controls.

"Yes. But it's the second pregnancy."

"She doesn't need to know that," I said, that fact having just been given to me.

"Actually, it *is* the sort of thing we ask about." The technician squeezed a neat line of gel on the transducer and half-swiveled back towards us. She paused, one hand on the keyboard of the ultrasound machine, one arm aloft above Pavia's belly. She planted her feet on either side of the stool as if bracing for impact.

"This will be a little cold." She slid back the sleeve of her lab coat and lowered her arm.

And up on the monitor we crash-landed into dark waters: a pulsing roar and the plankton streaming past, ghostly shapes— coral reef? shipwreck?—faintly visible in the agitated gloom.

"Let's try over here," the technician said, sliding the transducer over.

And there it was, moving jerkily like something caught in a net—something white, cartilaginous, huge-headed, human. It waved its arms and scissored its legs, the unconnected bones afloat inside, the fingers and toes offgassing from the hands and feet, and the striped ribcage with something boiling inside.

"Heartbeat is one-forty. Normal," said the tech.

The sound of the heartbeat, normal at a hundred and forty beats a minute, foamed in our ears like surf. Pavia had her hand in my hand and she gripped it hard. The articulate fetus scuttled sideways out of view.

Next the tech took some measurements, lite-brighting her way across the screen. I looked at Pavia lying on the table. I returned the hard squeeze of her hand, feeling for the metatarsals. What was inside her, really, that she could make this creature out of her own flesh, blood, genetic material?

"Things look fine," said our tech. "But I'll have the doctor come in, too. Do you want to know the sex of the baby?"

"Yes," Pavia said. I nodded.

More swooping and diving in the brine. "There," the tech said, twisting the transducer. "Can you see it?"

"Boy," Pavia murmured.

"Looks like." The tech slid the transducer into its holster and pushed down on her thighs as she rose from the stool. She grinned at us, turned, then left us alone in the dim room. The last shot of the fetus stayed on the screen, its tiny phallus like a sea plant anchored between its luminous legs.

Pavia hoisted herself up on her elbows and reached for a tissue. She blew her nose and lay back down with her arm over her eyes. This gesture of pathos, of course, would not be possible for someone with corrective lenses.

"You okay?"

She didn't say anything for a minute. "Yes," she eventuated, "There's a lot of moving parts." She sniffed. I waited.

"Spine, arms, head with that hingeing jawbone"—she waved her hand in front of her covered eyes—"kicking legs and Thea!" she said suddenly, like Helen Keller at the pump, getting

W-A-T-E-R after all. She threw her arm back and her eyes were open. "Thea, the heart." Her hand slid down to her chest; she was looking again at me.

"I know," I said, feeling a sudden arrhythmia of my own, "Whooshwhooshwhoosh. Going so fast."

"Like it's running. Like it's trying to overtake us already."

"Well he *is*," I said. I stared down at my sister in tragic repose, her gelled belly glistening like a new pearl in the gap between her sweater and her unzipped jeans. "He really is." That shut Pavia right up, and I went on.

"Whoosh," I said, leaning slightly toward her. "Whooshwhooshwhoosh."

At the café, pumped up by caffeine, the sense memory of Eli's erection against my waistband, and my sister's gratifying tears, I grabbed our paper cups and stuffed the napkins inside. "What about money for the baby?" I asked Pavia.

She and Jack weren't divorced, and so far, they hadn't worked out any of the details of their separation. With my help, Pavia was paying the mortgage on the townhouse. Jack had a place in a neighborhood near their work. I imagined it filled with laundry baskets of unwrapped client appreciation gifts—flashlight pens or inflatable neck pillows with the company logo—tags still attached.

Adeste fidelis
Laeti triumphantes

Pavia stood up and worked her arms into her long coat. "Well, by law Jack has to pay child support. But I don't know."

"Don't know what?"

"Jack does all right," she said, pushing open the glass door and heading into the crowded sidewalk. "But he's not rich."

"Neither are you."

"I know," Pavia conceded. "Anyway, his parents are rich. Maybe they should pay for it."

I had met Jack's parents, Ed and Nanette Reed, only once, at Pavia's wedding. They had white hair that evoked nature—snow, wind, clouds, fungus—and they were active types, people who likely took multivitamins and enjoyed long walks. They probably counted their financial advisor as a family friend. Of course, I had never had a real conversation with them. Pavia, I thought, loved them.

"If they hadn't read *A River Runs Through It*," Pavia was saying now, "They never would have sent Jack to college in Montana in the first place. We never would have met."

"So it's their fault?" Once again I found I was twisting idiotically as I walked, hustling to keep up with my long-legged sister. "And what are we even talking about, the baby or the divorce?"

"We're separated, not divorced."

"Do his parents know about the baby?"

Pavia nodded. "They're excited, Jack says. They think it will bring us back together."

"Will it?"

"I don't think so." She stopped to appraise a shoe display in a window, then pressed on. "I might never see them again."

"They're going to want to see the baby."

"I guess. But they hate me now. They're not going to see *me*." Pavia pulled her arms across her chest, hugging herself against the wind. "They wouldn't even miss the money, though." She tucked her chin down into her scarf.

The college crowd thinned as we walked on toward the townhouse, finally matching our strides. The snow was starting to stick on the sidewalks and parking meters, on the topsides of the bare tree branches. Pavia slowed down. Her gloved hand reached out to flick away the snow from each of the knobbed finials atop the wrought iron fence. *Flick. Flick. Flick.* She cleared her throat.

"I have an idea I want you to help me with. Ed and Nanette are coming back from Jamaica tomorrow to spend Christmas with Jack. I want to meet them at the airport."

"What kind of help?"

"Just come with me. I'm going to ask them about the money. For the baby. I need," she said, her voice rising as if at the end of a question, "I don't know. Just come with me, okay?"

"Okay."

We rounded the corner near Pavia's house. As the pale sun sank away, the street unspooled before us like archival film footage—brick sidewalks, hardwoods, lines of row houses all PBSed in blacks and whites—the scene's surface scratched and pocked by fast-falling snow.

"You know what's weird?" I said to Pavia. "Think about it: you have a penis inside you *all the time* now."

Pavia stopped walking. I followed her gaze.

A Jeep Eagle hatchback, grimy, double-parked, was idling at the curb near the front steps to the house. As we came closer, the bashed-in driver's side door swung open with a wrenching creak.

"Jesus Christ," I said, reaching for Pavia's wrist. "It's mom."

9. HOW TO USE A LADDER

One year when Dorothy was very sick and we girls needed to experience the cardiovascular, musculoskeletal, and psychosocial benefits of team sports, my sister and I were made to join the swim club. At the university pool, we swam every morning before school. Our coach was mean and mostly unseen; he sat in his glassed-in office off the pool deck and relayed his instructions through a microphone connected to the PA system.

Rogers, that's the kind of horseshit that'll get you disqualified. Two hands to the wall, goddammit. Rice, pick it up or go home. Turn it over, Boileau, turn it over. Turn it over. GodDAMmit. Turn. It. OVER.

The coach's voice slapped the wet tiles, echoed and amplified. He watched us from behind a window as unrevealing as a mirror. But I learned that if you were in the first lane, below the concrete lip of the pool's edge, he couldn't see you. Here, you could dive deep. You could pull the water past you in great round armfuls, heading down, and grab onto the bottom of the pool's ladder. You could hold yourself there, ears painful with the pressure, until the rushing silence became real and surrounding, like something you could breathe. Here, you could hold yourself like a spider in amber, a stillborn in the sac, preserving yourself for the future.

First, everyone says: *As Long as She's Healthy*. Then: *As Long as She's Happy*. As if these are modest hopes, reasonable bargaining points in a negotiation with management. *That's All We Ask!*

I'll tell you truthfully, my darling: these *are* too much to ask for. I'm sorry.

But come down. Come here. I can promise to give you this: an appetite for silence. Loneliness, and ways to find it when you need to. How to hold yourself safe, apart, tight to the lowest rung.

10. THE SECOND WIG

At the curb, our mother sat behind the glass in the passenger's side window, waiting. Joseph—tall, stooped, with a thin black ponytail discharging down his back—held up his palm at Pavia and me as he felt his way around the hood of the car toward the curb.

"Two sisters!" he cried. "Hello!" Joseph was about my age, though his face was creased and the skin on his cheeks was thick and pitted with acne scars.

He took a step toward us with his arms wide. Pavia stopped him by pointing her finger at the car's passenger door, behind which sat Dorothy, moon-faced and expectant, mouthing *Love you!*

Joseph turned with a giggle and pulled open the door. Dorothy hoisted herself out. It was revealed that she and Joseph were wearing matching blue tracksuits, stained in various places, white plastic zipper pulls shaped like lightning bolts. Together this time, they held out their arms to us.

Pavia and I set about embracing our visitors; I took Dorothy first. Out of the corner of my eye, I saw my sister lift her chin high over Joseph's shoulder, straining to avoid the starchy, cooked-noodle smell he and Dorothy shared after five days of sleeping in the car. We switched and hugged again.

"Wow," said Pavia adenoidally. "You made it."

"Of course!" Dorothy said. She smiled into the soft collar of her double chin, "You didn't believe me?"

"Joseph," I said to Joseph, who nodded happily, "I'm Thea. This is Pavia. Where's your stuff? How long are you staying?" I pulled open the car door and folded the front seat forward.

In the backseat, nestled among the empty tall boy cans of Natural Lite, were a duffle bag of clothes and two plastic grocery bags. I opened one of the bags, stirred its contents—loose tarot cards, matchbooks, packages of Corn Nuts and herbal cigarettes. Two issues of *Reader's Digest* bearing the subscription sticker from Dorothy's psychiatrist's office. Also: condoms, loose, individually wrapped.

"Sleeping bags are in the way back," Joseph was telling Pavia. "They're both mine."

Dorothy's jewelry box was in the second of the grocery bags. Pavia and I had given it to her as kids. The box was cardboard covered in pale blue pleather, embossed with a gold fleur de lis. I grabbed both bags and the duffle and backed my way out of the car, awkward as someone newly injured.

"Joseph, give me the car keys," Pavia said from the curb where she had successfully redistributed the sleeping bags to Dorothy and Joseph. "Thea, you take them up to the house. I'm going to find a parking place for your car, and then I'll be in." She waited for Joseph to put the keys into her outstretched hand, then turned away without meeting my gaze.

I led the way up the front steps, unlocked the locks to open the door, withstood General's usual greeting, and introduced the dog to Dorothy and Joseph. I wiped my shoes on the door mat—excessively, the way cartoon characters prepare to make a run for it—and then followed them inside.

"Whoa," Joseph said. He was standing in the hallway, looking up at the high ceiling, the long stairway going up to the second floor. "Echo!" he shouted.

Dorothy laughed and looked to me. I lurched past them into the living room and set their bags down on the pullout couch. I looked out the front windows. Where was Pavia, anyway—how long could it take to park the car? I saw two empty spaces on our street, but not the beat-up Eagle. A knocking in my chest started up then, deep and automotive-feeling, unsafe at any speed.

I turned around to face our visitors. "Have you guys eaten yet?" I asked, thinking, *Where is my sister, goddammit?*

They had no fixed plan, Dorothy and Joseph explained over the sauce-and-pasta I had peevishly prepared; they didn't want to be tied to a plan. By some occult New Age means they had begun to understand that they were meant to be with us at Christmas, that was all, and so they had come.

"It just felt right," Dorothy was saying yet again, "So I really wanted to. But Joseph made it happen."

"It's *your* car, Mom," I reminded her. "The car that brought you is yours." And on cue, we heard the front door open and shut, and Pavia re-entered the scene.

"We're in here!" I shouted to her in the hall. *Echo.* Pavia came into the kitchen looking newly weary.

"To get here I just followed the star in the East," Joseph continued happily, sliding out a chair for Pavia. He had had a shower and changed out of the tracksuit, into jeans and a health fair t-shirt, *Supernal Walks!*

"How old are you, anyway?" Pavia asked. She'd taken her seat and was holding her fork like a pencil over her plate, which I had filled for her fifteen minutes prior.

"Twenty-six moons. Twenty-six years young."

"You're Native American," Dorothy asserted to him unnecessarily, "Kootenai-Salish tribe." The lightning bolt on her zipper pull quavered as she sat up a little straighter in her chair and looked around to us, changed pronouns. "He's a very old soul." Creepily, this is what she used to say about me in parent-teacher conferences by way of explaining certain maladaptive behaviors, like my crouching in the janitor's closet during recess.

Pavia snorted. "You wrote that on our wedding card. About me and Jack."

"Yeah!" I sang, having had a bit to drink by then. Pavia back at home—and on my side, sounding like me?

"So Dorothy," I said, turning toward our shared progenitor, "Does everyone have one, an old soul? Doesn't anyone get to have a new one? Reduce, reuse, recycle?"

"How *is* Jack?" Dorothy asked Pavia, ignoring me. "Do you see him?"

Pavia chewed and chewed. She stared at Dorothy as if she (Dorothy) were the mouthful that was somehow resisting digestive enzymes.

"They're getting a divorce," Dorothy said sidelong to Joseph, who was spearing up pasta.

"Reduce, reuse, recycle," I suggested again.

"Shut up," Pavia said with her mouth full, pushing her chair back from the table. She swallowed and stood up. "Jack's fine. I spoke with him earlier today." She carried her plate to the sink and began rinsing it.

"Jack has an interesting path to walk," our mother said. "He's seeking himself in others."

"He's a salesman," Pavia called out with her back turned to us. "He's seeking commissions in others."

Dorothy narrowed her eyes visionarily. "I like him."

"I do, too," I said, surprising myself. I felt suddenly grateful to Jack for making me a better person, if only for a moment—the sort of person who pipes up with a good word for someone else.

"Great. Everybody likes Jack. We agree he's a gem." Pavia turned to face us. "I've got some work to do, so sorry—I'm going to ignore you all now. Thea, can you set them up? The couch pulls out."

Joseph helped me clear the table and wash the dishes. As we talked I learned that he and Dorothy had met at Supernal's downtown soup kitchen, the New Hope Center. On the advice of her mental healthcare provider, Rowan, she had decided to volunteer there. When she was feeling low, Joseph reported while water spilled over the plate in his hand, "your mother raised others up."

"How long did that last?" I asked. "The volunteering thing at the Center?"

Joseph twisted toward Dorothy, his back giving an audible pop. He sighed an ancient sigh. "I think—did you go two or three times, Dot?"

She didn't answer; with laboratorial concentration she was reaching for the stack of magazines piled on a table under the wall phone. Joseph turned back to me. "Then we met, and..." He set the dish in the drying rack, "New Hope. It was meant to be."

"He's a Gemini," Dorothy said.

"So you were a client?" I knew that was what you called the people who came to New Hope for meals. When I was in high school Rowan had made me volunteer there too. I lasted eight months, fueled by the image of myself providing succor to the needy and by the satisfying physical strain of my mute repetitions with the stew ladle. Of course the appeal wore off. I found it annoying to be told by the clients—senior citizens, homeless, people with serious challenges in the areas of self-regulation and personal hygiene—to cheer up. Wasn't that my line, after all?

"I was a client, mostly," Joseph said. "But I help out, too, when I can. I do some maintenance. They pay me."

"Alcoholic?"

Joseph nodded, smiled. "So I have to ask: Got any more beer?"

We did, and he and I each had one while we finished the dishes, and Dorothy sat at the table and alternated between reading *Us* and petting General's soft, furrowed brow. Joseph and I calculated that we had gone to high school together. Later, we moved to the living room and finished the beers. Dorothy went to the bathroom and stayed there.

"She's washing her hands in there," Joseph said, jerking his thumb toward the hallway bathroom. He slid down on the couch and put his feet up on the coffee table, gazing at his worn hiking boots in a concerned, pastoral way. "She'll be there for a while. She just…"

"Can't stop," I said. "I know. And do you know what that means?"

He burped, swallowed. "You want the diagnostic code?"

"It means she's headed back down," I said. "It means, my friend, that she won't be your happy little travel pal much longer."

Joseph shook his head. "Nah. She has social support now. She's eating better. She's taking ginseng." He sighed and sat up slowly, twisted his back to crack it again. "I *think* she's still taking ginseng…." He drifted back into the couch like an old soul, slowly transubstantiating into the cushions. For a while, we listened to the sound of the water running in the bathroom.

"She's going to get really down again," I lazily reemphasized. "Reduce, reuse, recycle."

"Right on," Joseph said. "I've been down myself. Down, down, down." His eyes were half-shut by now.

I looked at my fellow alumnus for a moment, then got up from the couch and went to lock the front door, turning off lights as I went. At the top of the stairs, Pavia's door was closed with no crack of light coming from beneath it. Dorothy came out of the bathroom. Her track pants swished once, twice, thrice as she toddled in the dark front hallway.

"Over there," I said. I pointed toward the living room like the Ghost of Christmas Yet to Come.

"Oh," said Dorothy. "Right."

Through the archway, we could see Joseph asleep on the couch, mouth open, hands in his lap.

"Thea," she whispered close to my face. "Thea, he's such a good friend to me. You know? I haven't had that for a long time."

Framed by the dark hallway, we were two profiles facing each other like souvenir silhouettes. I didn't want to hear about friendship or time. I didn't want to smell her breath with its faint hint of rhinovirus.

"Uh huh," I said.

"With Joseph, it's unconditional. He accepts me for who I am. Where I am. There's no judgment. You know?"

"Uh huh." It occurred to me that my recent history of moderate-to-heavy drinking had had the unexpected benefit of training me to keep my mouth shut when I was drunk. Or perhaps it was living with Pavia that had given me this surprising new discretion. I was still the insufferable kid who knew the answer in class—knew it urgently and absolutely, *better than anyone*—but I no longer felt compelled to raise my hand. I didn't really want to be called on anymore, it seemed. In the big city, was I growing up at last?

"And did he tell you?" Dorothy said, peering at me in the dim light. "He's Native American!"

"Right on," I said. Dorothy followed me into the front

room, where I shook Joseph awake with the heel of my hand. He and Dorothy stood off to the side while I pulled the bed out of the couch. As I dropped the folding legs down and tucked the sheet around the padding, General gave a little low bark. He was standing by the front door, wanting out.

So there I was a few moments later, standing on the front steps and watching the dog make small circles in the front yard with his nose to the ground. He found a suitable spot and crouched in that unstable, vulnerable way that big dogs do, eyes wide and alert, back legs trembling as if weakened by some dread muscle-wasting disease, polio or Duchenne's dystrophy maybe.

A car drove by. I looked at my watch. I looked at the black and purple sky. My mind made small circles. From the open door behind me—through which expensive heat escaped the house—I heard the springs of the hide-a-bed groaning as my mother settled on it. Did she expect me to come back to Supernal with her? Did she need me to? I shoved the thought aside.

General climbed the steps and sat down on my left foot. I stayed looking out at the street; I wondered what Eli was doing.

Elsewhere Eli was sleeping, dreaming an uncomplicated dream. He was happy without knowing it, I was sure. As in a vast plain, laying down with the lions and the lambs, he slept while serotonin washed across his brain folds like the waters of the Nile strumming the papyrus with a hushing sound, *the Nile, the Nile, the Nile*. Unconditionally and without judgment, he was sleeping, blind to me and mine.

The next morning Pavia knocked on my door early. It was time to go to the airport with her. As we left the apartment, we passed Dorothy and Joseph still asleep on the hide-a-bed. Joseph was curled in a fetal position; Dorothy was flat on her back, her breathing rattling up and down as on a weak and phlegmy ladder.

It was still dark outside; General's shitpile by the fence was frosted over. Pavia said, "No time to stop for coffee," before I had a chance to ask. We got in her car and in a few minutes the heater was blasting against my pants leg as we sped down the elevated highway over deserted, movie-set neighborhoods.

I looked out the window at the liquor billboards, the rows of three-family houses, the lack of available onstreet parking. I wondered, as I always do on drives through unfamiliar areas, what other people could possibly be doing, living there. What kind of jobs did they have? Where did they eat? Do they think about the people in cars flashing past their homes—fast as time and as glamorous in the abstract—and feel disappointed with themselves?

I rested my head on the window glass, blindly reading along my jawline with my fingertips, checking for untweezed chin hairs. "So how's this going to work, again?" I asked Pavia, who drove holding a candy cane between gloved fingers, licking it into a sharp white point. "With the Reeds, I mean?"

"I'm not sure," Pavia said. With her hair pulled back and dark lipstick on, she looked like a woman from a car ad, pan-European, ancestrally indifferent to public opinion. Speeding in the left-hand lane, we drew up behind a big blue Buick in which two elderly and hair-blurred heads bobbled above the seatbacks like loose Q-tips. Patiently and rhythmically Pavia pressed one black driving glove on the horn.

"This is going to be a play-it-by-ear kind of thing." She shifted in her seat as if to untuck her lungs from her thickening middle, "I'm going for—I'm thinking this can be a win-win."

I was skeptical, but the truth is, I had always trusted Pavia. And I didn't want to stop. "How's that?" I projected my voice over the sound of the car horn.

"There you go," she murmured as the Buick changed lanes ahead of us. "Look, everyone wants the same thing ultimately, right? A kid that's loved and well cared for, whatever happens? Wouldn't you want that?"

I blinked, sighed, turned on the radio. I didn't need to say anything. She pointed a pointy-gloved index finger at her purse, which was resting on the car floor by my feet.

"Check it out," she said.

I reached down and pulled the purse onto my lap and unclasped the middle part. I put my hand in; I lifted up a dry mesh scalp. The white hair growing out of it fell down in flattened half-curls around my wrist.

"It's a wig," Pavia said, glancing at it out of the corner of her eye as she bit down on the candy cane. "I'm wearing it at the airport."

I shook the thing as if to wake it up. "Okay," I said. I felt my jaw tightening up. I tried to imagine the good reason for a disguise. "But we're getting coffee first."

It was a Saturday and at that early hour the traveling public was in sparse attendance at the airport. Pilots and flight attendants, color coordinated in crisp uniforms, strode three and four abreast down the wide concourses, their wheeled luggage thrumming behind them on the linoleum. I was tailing my sister, trying to see Pavia as the flight crews might: *tall, dark haired, wearing a long coat and walking fast in high-heeled boots—a handsome woman. A woman whose lucky husband admires her and enjoys selecting fine jewelry for her, sometimes "just because." It says he'd marry her all over again. The way you might re-read a favorite book or a book that you didn't really understand the first time through.*

I decided yes, anyone would notice my sister. Admire her. Trust her. She was beautiful, poised, competent-seeming—it wouldn't occur to you that she was related to the other one, the one who trailed behind her with a Styrofoam cup held aloft and leaking visibly down her wrist.

Pavia turned her head to me. "Come on. They're almost landing now." She pulled her purse across her stomach and walked faster.

The Reeds lived in a nearby suburb with a springer spaniel and now, two days before Christmas, they were returning from Jamaica. No doubt they were returning with colorful local handicrafts—a tiny knitted vest in Rastafarian colors for the baby?—and a camera full of pictures of themselves with their arms slung around their new pals, the bus driver and pool boy. The Reeds were like that, I had inferred over time; they were interested, sincere, and appreciative. Like Jack, who was one of them, of course.

And then just ahead of us on the concourse as we drew near the security gate, there was Jack's back. He was standing with his hands in his pockets, looking up at the arrivals screens in a way that gave him a slight overbite, an innocence. Pavia quickly veered left toward the women's bathroom, and motioned for me to follow.

Tucked inside the little alcove by the bathroom, Pavia sat down in the first of three banged-up wheelchairs parked next to the drinking fountain. She flipped the metal footplates down and in with her boots. She reached inside her purse and handed me the wig and a pair of oversized Yoko Ono sunglasses, black and caliper-like at the temples.

"I know these are ugly," she said warningly. "Don't say it."

I did exactly as my sister told me. I put the glasses on and began stuffing her hair inside the wig. She wriggled and readjusted in the wheelchair seat, pulling her long coat out and away from her body. I held onto her head. When she was still again I grabbed a front section of wig hair and yanked it forward like a ripcord; the wig was finally on.

"Okay," Pavia whispered. She took out another pair of sunglasses—identical to the ones she'd given me—and pushed them on. Then she patted the armrests impatiently. "Let's go!"

I grasped the molded handles of the chair and leaned forward. Jaw clenched, I began to push. My nose was near her desiccated pseudo-hair. "Okay," I mouth-breathed through my teeth as we rolled forward, "Okay. But tell me—*now* Pavia—what are we doing?"

Pavia waited while a woman's voice announced the flight's arrival over the P.A., then while the voice repeated the announcement more slowly, extra soothingly, with odd emphases: *That's flight SEVEN sixty-nine, with SERVICE from Miami, arriving AT gate twenty-two.*

I'd marry her ALL OVER AGAIN, I thought, wishing I were anywhere else.

"I just need to see Ed and Nanette first, before I ask for the money. For just one last time, and I don't want..." Pavia gestured outward from her wheelchair seat, "I don't want to see the fake expression they're always going to have when they see me from now on."

"Like...like what expression?" I asked. What was my sister doing? I felt huge and remote in my rectangular sunglasses, like someone trying to reach a distant canister of bacon bits from behind a salad bar sneezeguard.

"Like they *like* me," she said. "Faking it. Like how Jack still looks at me. Anyway, it's just for a second. Just for one last look. We can follow them to the baggage claim, and we'll take this stuff off, I'll talk to them there."

She reached up with two gloved hands and slapped at her

wig. "Please," my sister said, "Please, let's *go*."

So I wheeled her out into the concourse, stopping where the carpet began in front of the security gate. Passengers were filtering through the doors already, melanin-dappled and exhausted, burdened with carry-ons and walking in the defeated way of people returning from indulgent vacations.

I spotted Ed and Nanette. Truly, they too wore matching sweat suits; pale blue, unstained. Their eyes passed over Pavia and me like waves on smooth sand, and retreated. They didn't recognize us.

Then they saw Jack. And all at once Ed's lined face was drawn smooth with a wide smile and Nanette was rushing forward, her arms shooting up into the air. Her tote bag fell off her shoulder, knocking her briefly to one side; Ed put his hand on her back to steady her. She kept coming forward toward her son and then Ed began to laugh with a deep and booming laugh as they all came together, and as Jack put his mother inside his open arms, and as his head bent down to hers, and as his face and mouth were saying *Mom* and other things as his father laughed again and the crowd curved and flowed around the three of them, diverted.

Pavia and I were fifteen feet away from all this, this reunion of the Reeds. I was twisting the wheelchair handles, revving silently as I watched them. And then I looked away. The other passengers came at us like nothing. Pavia sat still as a prop in front of me, her wig like a dirty lather on top of her head. I realized, with a sharp, angina-like pain that I was the one with the handles in my hand, and it was my job to take my sister away.

So I backed the chair up and we followed the crowd back down around the concourse. At the baggage claim I just kept pushing, past the luggage carousels and out the glass door to the street. Pavia stood up and followed me to the parking garage. Neither of us said anything all the way home. Parallel parking in front of the townhouse, I wrenched the steering wheel back and forth, hitting the curb repeatedly with the tires. Then my sister said aloud, finally, "I don't need their fucking money anyway," and I pulled hard on the wheel again and agreed through gritted teeth, wholeheartedly.

Dorothy and Joseph slept through our return from the airport and the ringing of the phone. It was Eli calling, and later when he came over I kissed him at the door abruptly.

"Sorry!" I said, embarrassed. I licked my chapped and slightly fraying lips, pulled off a strip of skin with my fingers. "Poky, huh? I guess I'm some sort of thistle."

Eli took my face in his hands, stroked my earlobes with his thumbs. "Defer to the plant professional," he said. A second, a minute, a whole year passed. "You're a kind of rose," he said at last, and kissed me carefully, again.

We took a commuter train out to the suburbs and brought home a three-foot Christmas tree, holding it on our laps like smug parents of a well-behaved toddler. We put the tree in the townhouse, in the front room next to the TV, and Eli stayed and helped decorate it. We made paper chains out of the glossy pages of Pavia's company's annual report from the previous year, and Joseph used the kitchen shears to cut a star out of a beer can. Dorothy sat on the couch, occasionally offering suggestions for ornament symmetry which we all ignored. Everyone but Pavia got more or less drunk, and Eli stayed overnight for the first time.

In my room, having sex in silence and full overhead light, we wound together as in a time-lapse nature film, Technicolor and surprising, two comic botanicals weaving upward so at last my tears of choked-back laughter ran down into my hair and ears.

"My mom really likes you," I told Eli later that night in my room, sitting up and tightly grabbing the toes of one of his feet. I began to try to crack them each in turn.

"Ouch," he said. "Jesus." He smiled. "Is it the Virgo thing?"

"No. She just likes you."

"Doesn't she like everyone though?"

"Well, yeah."

Eli wrenched his toes free and threw both legs around my waist in a leg lock. "That's a cool way to be."

It wasn't a cool way to be, I knew, but I liked it so much, being caught like that, pinned by him to the mattress. It felt specific and conditional, intentional, point-earning. His femoral-pulse thrummed reliably against my hip. I closed my eyes and felt its beat and allowed myself to speculate: Maybe I and Christmas and everything might be all right after all that year. Perhaps the people of my family had managed to discover—just in time—our unifying aesthetic: a lovable dysfunction, the kind people write about?

I doubted it, wished it, fell asleep doing so in Eli's weird embrace.

The next day Eli went home to Indiana. Pavia and I both took a few days off work, and as a way of getting Dorothy and Joseph out of the house for at least a few hours each day, we did a lot of scheduled errands. Pavia bought them both clothes at an outlet store, for one thing. We took them to the museum where we shuffled through the rooms with our coats in our arms, feeling stunned and excluded by color fields and high concepts. We went daily to the grocery store where of course we bought a lot of alcohol, which in turn necessitated trips to the recycling center fifteen miles outside of the big city.

Pavia, Joseph, and I loved the recycling center. We loved throwing the glass bottles into the bins. It had the excitement of special effects, domestic violence, parties ending badly. We threw green, brown, clear glass——each in its proper bin—and we celebrated the whack, the smash, the shards falling like a beautiful killing rain. I loved the feel of the cold necks in my hand, just before I let them fly. We were saving the earth! Reduce, reuse, recycle! Merry Xmas!

Yet at the recycling center Dorothy never heard our shouts of displaced eco-joy. She stayed dozing in the car. She'd begun her downward slide.

On Christmas Eve I cooked a ham. Dorothy, who had been sleeping in the front room all day until dinner was ready, sat between me and Joseph at the table. He was wearing the white wig of Pavia's he had found in the telephone book drawer. He stood up to make a toast.

"Peace," he said, looking at us seriously, one at a time. "And for Dorothy, *suuntsaa.*" He drained his glass, and sat heavily back down.

Dorothy smiled at him incuriously. She reached up and pulled the wig off his head, then tossed it in the kitchen corner with General. She took a slice of ham off her plate and threw it, too, onto the floor.

"*Suuntsaa,*" Dorothy told the dog. "That means love, in Shoshone."

Suddenly a chair fell over with a crash. And we saw that Pavia was on all fours on the tile. She was scrambling with General with her head down, her hair around her face.

"NO!" she yelled at the dog, and she pulled her hand back just as General snapped. I jumped up from my chair and all at once Pavia was standing too, her fist clutching the slice of ham, one knee hitched up to show the sole of her shoe to General. He growled at her.

"You think I'm rich?" Pavia shouted at Dorothy. She was

panting. She put her foot down. "You think it's okay to waste food?"

She stomped to the sink and switched on the disposal. We heard the wet, shredding sound as the ham was done away with. I looked at Joseph, who looked back at me with the pure sadness of the uninvolved.

"I don't think you're rich," our mother said. "I'm sorry." I couldn't look at her, of course, but I saw Pavia doing it and staying mad. Pavia wiped her hands on a yellow dishtowel, then draped it from the edge of the counter like a stage curtain pulled closed.

"Good night," my sister said as she turned and swept past us out of the kitchen, and we echoed it back to her in a chorus —"'Night!"—all of us sounding sore, afraid.

The next morning I woke up when Pavia pushed my door open. She was leaning against the doorframe wearing pale blue pajamas, the waistband low under her belly like a gunslinger's belt.

"Guess what?" she asked, sticking a fist into her newly padded hip. "Joseph is gone." She gave me a lazy smile. "And he took Mom's jewelry, and a bunch of her other stuff, too."

I threw back the cover. "Merry fucking Christmas," I said, and Pavia gave her imitative laugh again.

11. LET'S NOT NOT KNOW

You have a vagina and please: it's not a general region. It's not just *down there*, or just your privates. And despite what they will probably tell you at daycare, it's not your pee-pee. That refers to something else—you'll learn this on your own, as soon as you discover a way to reach that region. So let's be specific, just as your body is specific—or will be eventually, anyway—containing two hundred and six bones, ten visceral organs, and sixty thousand miles of blood vessels. Let's not not know. Because you do.

That is the vulva. It's the fatty part on top, cushy, separate at the bottom. Starts out bald; gets hair later.

Here is (are) the labia, the fleshy curtains you can draw to each side....

...ta-da! That's the urethra. If you insist, *that* is the pee-pee.

And that is the clitoris. O nucleon, keloid, tapioca bead! O lemondrop, dot matrix, glycosylated tack. Take your time learning about the clitoris, customize your approach; its job is joy.

Finally, *that* is the vagina. Simply an opening and a long, smooth slide. A letdown, if you will. If a baby is in your tummy—

your uterus, I mean—and wants to get out, here is the way it comes. And yes, of course, when it comes, someone must be there to catch it.

12. WHITE LADY ON A RED BACKGROUND

So on that Christmas morning I followed Pavia downstairs. In the living room, the foldout bed had been put away. I saw Dorothy's blue jewelry box on top of the coffee table and tucked it under my arm. Then we went into the kitchen where we found Dorothy already dressed, tugging on a drawer handle with both plump hands.

"Coffee filters?" she asked as we came in the room. Pavia went over and yanked the drawer open, reminding me of a recent medical case in which a twenty-three-year-old man had fractured his C5 and C6 vertebrae forcing open an old window. There had been devastating neurologic consequences, vasomotor and trophic changes as sequelae....

"Thanks." Dorothy sat slowly down at the table. "And Merry Christmas, girls."

I sat down in the chair next to her. I tried this: I let my head rest on my mother's shoulder. We watched Pavia fold the filter and throw scoops of coffee grounds into it. "What happened to Joseph?" I asked.

"Well," Dorothy said, "It looks like he's gone." I lifted my head and she smiled gently at me. Her tired blue eyes held mine like a pair of soft hooks until I looked away.

"Where?" I asked. "How long? Did he leave a note?"

"He's like that, Thea. When it's time to go, he goes."

"With your stuff?"

Dorothy shook her head. I put the jewelry box on the table in front of her.

"Nothing in it," I said, opening the lid and presenting the inside to her, game-show style.

"Sweetie." Dorothy reached up to take a mug of coffee from Pavia. Her hands trembled as she tore open a bag of Sweet and Low and stirred it in with her spoon. "Honey. There was nothing in there to begin with."

"What are you talking about? You had...things. You had a pearl necklace, your wedding ring, that cameo ring—you know, that lady's face...?" I turned my head and pointed at my profile, pushed up my glasses. "The white lady on a red background. The ring. The one you said you'd give to me."

"And Grandma Alva's rings," Pavia said, leaning against the counter and crossing her arms above her belly. "Remember those?"

Dorothy was stirring her coffee around and around. For a full minute and with an almost ecstatic effort of restraint I waited for her to say anything. Her spoon ground around the bottom of the mug with the sound of a failing manual transmission.

"So what about it, Mom," I said, finally reaching over and taking the spoon out her hand. "What about all of your jewelry?"

She raised the mug and spoke above its rim. "All those things have been gone for a while now," she said. "We pawned them to buy gas to come out here. And most of everything else—like the duffle bag and boom box?—that was his."

I looked at Pavia, who had begun to rub her eyes with her fingers. "So, okay," she said in a muffled voice from behind her hands. "You get social security, right? Money from Dad? And I sent money, right?"

"That's right." Dorothy spoke precisely, as if under oath, the coffee mug still pressed to her lower lip.

Nobody said anything. Dorothy blew on her coffee.

"Then what the hell, Mom?" I snapped the jewelry box closed. "Where has all your money been going? It's not like Pavia has money to burn," I swung my arm toward Pavia. "You may have noticed that she's pregnant? Jack is gone? The baby will cost money? And you know what else?"

I opened the jewelry box and let the hinges snap the lid down again. I did this two more times; the box jawed the empty air. "You know what else? We gave this jewelry box to you for a reason."

I paused again; what was the reason? Anyway, I went on: "We got it for you when we were kids, Mom! Kids give stuff to their moms, right?"

Time roared hot in my ears; I was sliding backwards, not to that specific sentimental scene but something near it, some sequela. "It's supposed to hold things. It's supposed to be where you keep things that are special. Things that are special *to you*."

One, two, three seconds passed.

"I know that, Thea," Dorothy said. She put the mug down at a tilt, spilling coffee on the table. "But we were trying to get out here to see you. I missed you."

She looked at me and her face—full and horribly open—was like a basin about to spill over; I felt I would drown if it did. Carefully, I reached for a napkin. I slid it forward so its corner soaked up the spilled coffee on the table. My mother and I watched it do its little job there, perfusing brown.

"Hey," Pavia said then. She had both hands on the right side of her stomach and was looking down.

"Baby. Baby's moving! Here." She walked her fingertips back and forth, tracking it from above. "Come feel it, Thea, Mom."

Maybe Dorothy hadn't heard. She pushed herself to her feet and looked at us blankly. "I think I'll lie down for a while. Can you wake me when it's time to open presents?" And she moved past us out of the kitchen.

So I stood up and put out my hands to Pavia. I pressed them to her hardening stomach and waited. Then I felt it: a small, rolling thump.

No, I didn't feel it. I heard it with my hands—a sound lost inside a drum. It was impossible to believe that it would ever find its way out.

"Did you see about the TV?" Pavia asked softly by my ear, scooping her thumb inside her bare navel to wipe out the lint, "Joseph took our TV, too."

Later on Christmas day, because Dorothy stayed in the foldout couch next to the tree, Pavia and I opened our presents at the kitchen table. I received a sweater and a set of expensive skincare products from Pavia. I got a bookstore gift certificate from Walter. Eli gave me a framed photograph of a child's elephant-shaped watering can lying at the bottom of a window well.

From Joseph, Pavia and I were surprised to find a note, written on the white side of some Santa Claus wrapping paper, folded up and tucked in the spout of the milk carton inside the refrigerator.

Sisters, it began.

Be good to your mother. She is a good person and she loves you.

Peace to you all.
Joseph

The next day, Pavia gave her hair a hot oil treatment, took a long shower, then called Walter.

"Daddy," she said when he answered, and then he said something back and she laughed a real laugh.

Pavia paced the apartment with the phone to her ear, tapping the walls rhythmically with her knuckles as she went. I sat at the table reading the paper and missing the TV. Pavia was telling Walter about Dorothy—*tanked, crashed, broke*, she was saying—and then she was saying less, as Walter was talking.

In the newspaper, cops and firemen handed out toys to needy children. The President, god's proxy, blessed our country. Black ice was responsible for deaths of holiday travelers; critics picked their early Oscar favorites; a capsized ferry resulted in the death of sixty Bangladeshi wedding celebrants. Then in real life Pavia was standing next to me, pushing the phone into the side of my head and saying, "Dad wants to talk to you."

I sat back in the kitchen chair. "Hi," I said.

My father coughed for a while. "Same to you. Merry fucking Christmas."

Suddenly I really missed him. I wanted to be back in his house in Supernal, pajama-bound, watching the sky steadily shed snow on the roofs and fences, on the disappearing ground. I wanted to sit at the kitchen table and do the crossword with him, taking drags off of his filterless cigarette.

"So listen, Thea. Pavia hasn't told you this yet, but you're going to have to bring Mom home."

One, two, three seconds passed. My mouth felt like an open hole in the front of my face.

"No fucking way. " I glared toward Pavia, who was loading the dishwasher. "No. Anyway, I have to work. There's a module I have to get out the door."

"A what?"

"A learning module! For nurses! On pressure ulcers!"

"Bullshit." Walter dryly inhaled from his cigarette. "Take a few days off."

"Why not Pavia?" Then, recklessly, "Why not *you*?"

My father laughed, which started another coughing spasm. "Your sister's pregnant, so that's out. And you know that I don't do that."

I did know that; he wouldn't do more. Over the years, much like the body moves to contain a staph infection by creating a hardened mass of tissue over the insult, Walter had tried to wall himself off from Dorothy. It didn't work. After their separation he stayed married. He gave her money and talked to her on the phone and drove her to the doctor and visited her up at the house and she was always worse. She would cry. She kept the house dark. Sitting in her white-going-gray nightgown she wanted to talk and talk. Or she stayed in bed and was silent, empty plates on the floor, old toast, used tissues, spoons, notes, lists. *You left me*, Dorothy would never say to Walter. Why would she? He had taken just one thing for himself—the chance to move out—and no one blamed him. After all, he wasn't going to be happy.

"You're up," Walter said into the phone. "And look, Thea. Don't bitch about it. It'll only be five days."

Five days; I couldn't think about five days and all the thinking that comes with driving across the country, or the five days of *not* thinking, with my mother silent beside me.

"What happens when I get there?"

"I'll fly you back to the big city."

Fly back. Okay. I worked my jaw a bit, as if checking a post-fight injury. "What happens to her, then? You going to take care of her?"

"We'll see," Walter said. "I don't know. I'll stay with her for a few days to see what to do. Goddammit."

With a pen I began to draw circles in the margins of the newspaper next to the headline *Newborn Males' Testicle Woes Linked to Soy.* "She hates the hospital," I said, and immediately wished I hadn't. "This really sucks, Dad."

"And it's all your fault."

"I know!" I laughed gratefully. "She should never have had us kids!"

"You're telling me." I pictured him grimacing, and his eyes—one green and one brown—narrowing beneath his long eyelashes. Once upon a time, five days or thirty years ago, he would have been so handsome; even, I thought semi-creepily but not abnormally I suppose, my type of guy.

"We pushed her over the edge, huh?" I went on. "Little babies on fat feet, toddling on toward the precipice and—"

"Shut up," my father interrupted. "All the blame is mine and I'm not going to talk about it. Now shut up and say goodbye."

I did both, abruptly. I hung up the phone. One, two, three minutes passed while my thoughts settled about me like particles of dust....

Pavia had gone upstairs and the apartment was soundless, still as an empty exhibit. I looked up at the ceiling, cracked and far away, and at the chandelier with its octet of burnt out, flame-shaped bulbs. It was too hard to get up there to replace them; that had been Jack's job. I registered the lack of everyday urban sounds outside: no bus, no garbage pickup, no car alarms, no boom boxes. It was still the day after Christmas. I reminded myself that I was simply in a gap—like the space between sofa cushions, or the summer hiatus where no new TV episodes are on, or the cognitive pause of a petit mal seizure—and I reminded myself that it would end or close or I would get out somehow, and soon. It was just a matter of time and endurance. So I knew this, and so I could let the quiet fill me up till I was empty to the very top, and cold.

I sat there for a while. The phone rang; it was Eli calling from Indiana.

It was starting to get dark outside and I could see my reflection in the kitchen window, double-paned; I was blurry edged, slightly off-register, like a 3-D movie without the glasses. How will I remember this Christmas, I wondered?

Eli told me the time his flight returned to the city, and I told him about Joseph leaving, and about Pavia's baby—"Quickening," he said, enjoying the word as he should, a word as special as an annual holiday—and I told him about the road trip I had to take with Dorothy and that I'd be back after New Year's.

"When do you leave?" he asked. "And, hey—do you want me to come with you?"

And there I was again in the window reflection, Girl on Phone, Long-Distance; Christmas 1993. And there I was cold, cold, smiling, saying no.

How will I remember this Christmas? I had wondered at that moment. Well, now we know.

Two days later, after I had arranged for extra time off work and after Dorothy's car had been tuned up by Pavia's usual mechanics up the street—identical Portuguese twins with Carhartt overalls and a shared unwillingness to replace anything that hadn't actually fallen off the car—I set out for Supernal with Dorothy.

"You'll be fine," Mauritzio had said, folding his thick forearms across his chest, "and if you're not..." Marcelo finished his brother's sentence—"Pffft"—with a noncommittal shrug of his rounded and presumably hairy shoulders.

"Pffft," I said later, as I turned up the onramp to the highway. Dorothy sat in the passenger seat with her hands on her thighs and a look of perfect equanimity on her face. She gazed out the window as the city sank away and I accelerated across two lanes. She was completely inside her depression by now, nearly catatonic, but no one would know this by looking at her—not the toll booth guy in the beginning of the trip, or the Triple A members whose cars passed ours along the way, or the families at the gas stations where we stopped, or the acne-chinned college students who manned the night desks at the Motel 6s we stayed in. Slo-mo and placid, eating cashews one after the other from the jumbo Mr. Peanut can on her lap, she looked imperially satisfied, almost smug, and I hated this as if it were real. I wanted to get to Supernal as soon as I could, and I wanted to see Walter coming down the porch steps as I pulled in. I wanted to see his face as he calculated, with one look at Dorothy, how far I had come.

Of course I did all the driving, and we took five days to get to Supernal. And nothing happened along the way except one thing, in Nebraska. And it was no big deal and it couldn't be helped, but I still think about it. And when I do, that one thing—one small event buried in the middle of the trip with all its long days, dull croplands, bad radio, poor lumbar support—it comes back weirdly articulate, consistently, like the *60 Minutes* stopwatch detailing time.

What happened was that an animal—medium-sized, dog-shaped—appeared at the side of the road and then plunged forward. It had an oversimplifying urgency attached to its movement, the way a road flare loses its pink head in a stiff wind. I saw it and I could have swerved or braked, maybe, before it slid beneath my mother's car and became, at that moment for me, a bodily sensation, a consequence occurring in the abdomen distinctly—a pill being swallowed in one gulp, the bass drum's quick contribution to the punch-line (ba-DUM-bump), a kind of quickening. It was like a sick joke, too easy, irresistible. And when I looked in the rearview mirror I saw it behind us in uneven silhouette, ridged and purpled like a set of knuckles stuck to the road, *Black Power*.

And I looked over at my mother next to me; she was turned toward the passenger side window. Didn't she feel it? What was she staring at out the window? You could jab your fingers into those two eyes and she wouldn't see any less. The adrenaline began to come like anger in the cartoons, a climbing redness filling in from the bottom all the way up to my clear and bulbous head, the sweat jumping out of my hands like straightpins onto the steering wheel, and my mind grabbing for something....

A story. Out of luck, under a spell, denied a rightful inheritance? Practically everything can be solved by a journey, I had learned from stories. And after the adventure, after the educational exile, the peasant always returns to restored peace in the kingdom, whereupon a communal sigh of relief caresses the land like a benevolent wind.

"Pffft," I said, exhaling the breath I'd held and modeling a Mediterranean fatalism and ancient belief in *destino*. The animal I'd just killed—whatever it was—was now only a spot on the highway. It was, I told myself, already small and getting smaller and smaller. It was coagulable, solvent, self-limiting. No one was going to blame me forever.

13. ADVICE FOR IF YOU'RE UGLY

It may turn out that you are burdened, like your mother, with a long equine face and an abundance of body hair. You may require corrective lenses that over time will leave a salmon-colored dent on each side of your nose. You may smile too widely and in general be a person whose facial expressions betray a certain emotional lability.

If so, buck up. People—especially boys if they have a sense of humor and are at least partially inclined toward girls, sexually speaking—won't mind as much as you think. With your looks, you likely won't disappoint in bed or worry about losing them (your looks, I mean) or, worse, implement desperate measures—heavy makeup comes to mind—to prevent same. Your "good features" will receive abundant praise, and you'll feel free to dress in an "interesting" way. Compared to beautiful girls, you'll get less shit, I should imagine, and more personal space.

But what if you find, some time into the project of growing up, that you are spiritually unattractive? That you have in yourself a surplus of rage, bitterness, envy? A lack of understanding, a lack of hope for change? A heart that's dense and inward, small and tight, wedged inside your ribcage the way a blackhead packs a pore?

I don't know. I don't. Here's what they told me:

Love is never having to say you're sorry.

Love is letting go.

Love is a verb, not a noun.

Love is a verb? Fine. You might try what I tried, then. Conjugate.

14. SUPERNAL INVERSION

Dorothy and I arrived at Walter's house in Supernal on New Year's Day. An inversion lay over the valley like an overfull lint screen, lending a strange and muffled coziness to the town. It had only been four months since I was last in my hometown, but already it felt pretend to me, with its bars advertising video poker and karaoke, its student-discount tanning salons, its acres of slush-filled parking lots half-full with pickups and dented muscle cars. What do people do here?

I turned the car this way and that down the tree-lined streets, heading toward the public library and Walter's house next to it. He'd been renting it for more than a decade, ever since the day that Dorothy had thrown his clothes out onto the lawn of our house in the suburbs.

He needed, she'd insisted that spring day, to See And Honor The Goddess In Her. And When He Had Done So, she had declared, standing on the concrete steps wearing a batik halter-top sundress—inside which her large breasts joggled, suggesting colonial unrest—then and only then Would He Be Permitted To Return.

I was outside with Walter that day, and I had begun to grab up his underwear and socks with a vermin-like intensity, stuffing them as fast as I could into a black plastic garbage bag. I couldn't look up—it was five thirty at night and neighbors were coming home from work, tapping their brakes as they drove past our house and peering at us indiscreetly, no doubt, as I myself would have done. So I didn't see Walter's face when Dorothy gave him her ultimatum. But I heard his reply.

"Fine," he'd said, and the syllable was deep with fury and ringing with unalloyed joy. He had it at last: permission to leave. He turned to me then and held out his hand for the garbage bag. I'd tied a knot at the top of it and handed it over. He'd walked to the Jeep Eagle—our family had just bought it from his boss Judith—and thrown the bag in the passenger's seat.

"Thea. Call and tell your sister what's going on." Pavia was a sophomore at the university then and lived in a sorority house downtown. "I'll meet you at her place in a couple of hours, and we'll figure out the car."

He'd dug in his coat pocket for the car keys, then given me a look of understanding, which was the worst part. What was he understanding? Of course, by now I know that such a look nearly always signals absence. Shit out of luck, it means.

I'd turned back to look at Dorothy. Arms akimbo, my mother was arranging the elements of her face into the world's first smile—primitive, imperfectly balanced—an awful, female monument. She didn't understand either.

"Fine," she echoed from within that smile. To her right, under the dirty picture window at the front of the house, a decade's worth of cigarette butts and chewed gum—a trove of familial DNA there—was scattered across the hard dirt like artifacts. She was haughty as a goddess with that smile on her mouth, and when I met her eyes I began to turn to stone.

"Later, Thea," Walter said, and he got in the car and drove away.

"Later, Thea," I murmured to myself ten years later as I pulled into the driveway at Walter's house and got out of the car. I walked stiffly around to Dorothy's side and lifted the dented door up on its hinges so I could open it. I held out my hand and pulled my mother out of the car the way one weighs an anchor. And then we were standing there in the driveway as the front door opened, and for me it was a little like being home. For Dorothy? I think it wasn't like anything. She was beyond simile—somewhere I never go, obviously—flatlining utterly (figuratively speaking) saying nothing, nothing, nothing.

Walter came out of the house without a coat, wearing a thin white t-shirt and sweatpants, moccasin slippers. He kissed me on the cheek.

"Thanks," he said to the side of my face.

"Hello," Dorothy said. "Quite a drive." She smiled at Walter as if her face were made of heavy canvas. He kissed her on the forehead, and held her hand as we went up the sidewalk and into his house. He got her a glass of water while I lay down on the floor in his front room.

"Quite a drive," I heard her say again from the kitchen. I heard the glass being put back on the counter. "I think I'll take a nap."

Lying on the floor, looking at the screws on the underside of Walter's scarred coffee table, I listened to the floorboards squeak as my parents made their way down the hall. I heard the door to his bedroom stick, then open. I felt the floor jump when Walter threw something heavy off the bed—probably some books—to make room for her. Hypersomatosensitive after 120 hours in the car with my mother, I registered every vibration in the house as if

I, spider-like, had spun its frame out of my own abdomen. I knew when Dorothy had dropped her shoes and then was in bed, and when she turned over on her side and was going to stay there in that position. And then, with Walter's heavy footfalls coming back down the hall, I let myself relax.

He came and stood over me. "I can't get down there, so you come up here. Let's have a smoke." He held out his hand to help me up. "You going up to her place tonight?"

I sneezed from the floor dust as he pulled me to my feet. "No way," I said. Dorothy's house—my childhood home—was in a suburb on the edge of town, a development with a lighted sign at the entrance—*Brookside,* fluorescent—and consisting of 50 poorly built ranch-style homes, each with a picture window in front, 3 bedrooms off the main hall, and wall-to-wall Berber carpeting throughout. "No one coming off an interstate should be exposed to so much sameness. I'm staying here," I said. I wiped my glasses on my sweatshirt as I followed Walter to the kitchen.

"Enjoyed the trip, then, did you?" In the kitchen, Walter poured two cups from his ancient and stained Mr. Coffee maker. He gave me the one in my favorite mug, the pale blue one, and we sat down at the card table in his dining room.

I looked around. This is how my father's house has looked ever since he moved in: Walls painted white over layers of rippled wallpaper. High ceilings, with cobwebs looping from the light fixtures. Windows, loose or painted over, that take on frost in the winter. Books stacked on crates and on wheeled carts from the library, and some folding chairs and a Lionel Trains calendar on the wall in the kitchen. From the archway I could see back into the living room with its worn leather chair and a coffee table. I could see the couch for which I have always had real affection tinged with pity, and which I treat with deference as you would an elderly Russian aristocrat—a distant Romanov relation perhaps—as it is upholstered in green velvet with a peony pattern, and because it is extra-long and slightly uncomfortable, clearly meant for another time and another kind of living. We had had the couch up at Dorothy's—it had been Alva's. We used to wake up and see Walter sleeping on it there.

Walter shook a cigarette out of the pack on the table and lit it with a match. He inhaled, coughed, handed the cigarette to me and said, "So tell me about your sister."

I knew he would ask this, and I knew what it meant. Why had Pavia left Jack, he wanted to know, and how was she going to manage on her own, and was she all right? I was ashamed that even though I lived with my sister, I didn't know the answer to any of these questions. Luckily, I had worked up a plausible account.

"She's fine," I began. I took a puff off his cigarette and blew it out quickly. "The baby seems to be good; did Pavia tell you it's a boy?"

Walter nodded, shrugged, and waited. I parked the cigarette in the clay ashtray I'd made for him in grade school, a circular tray with a peace sign scratched into the bottom.

"And she'll keep working of course, and her job is going great. They just expanded the leadership training she was doing; now everybody in the corporation is going to get it. She'll do some traveling for the rollout or whatever, but only for the next month or so."

"Everybody gets leadership training? Everyone's a leader?"

"It's called Self-Leadership." Seated at the table I could look through a set of poorly hung French doors into the small fenced backyard. There were a few twisted breadcrumbs frozen into the old snow outside; as usual Walter was overfeeding the local fauna.

"Self-Leadership is like, how to inspire and motivate yourself, I think. How to show initiative and proactivity, even if you're not a manager. How to model values and manage time."

"How not to cheat on your timecard."

"Yeah. And being your own best friend. And being the peace you seek in the world. And not hiding your light under a bushel."

Walter smiled. "I can see it. She can really do it, can't she? Your sister can say absolutely anything."

"Well, she's pretty. And people just like her. Whatever she says, they think, 'I'll have what she's having.'" Our eyes met, and we shook our heads a little, like a pair of those toy dogs on a dashboard, ever so slightly incredulous.

"I mean, she doesn't have to do anything, you know?" I continued. "She's always getting job offers from other companies, and raises, and...stuff."

"Stuff," Walter grunted. "Goddamn. Nobody else in the family can make money for shit."

"I know. Maybe she's our ration of it. She can just show up in her nice clothes with her nice face, and her success is already decided. She can't fail if she tries."

Walter took a sip of his coffee. He picked up the newspaper and folded it back so the crossword was on top. He didn't look up as he spoke.

"Is that what she's trying to do, then? After all? She's trying to fail?"

I hadn't thought of that, actually. I watched Walter push the heel of his hand across the newspaper fold one last time, pick up his pen. I watched him begin to fill in the squares of the crossword.

"I guess," I said slowly, apoxically. Besides feeling stupid, I was struggling to imagine what it must feel like to have to try to be imperfect. *Snow falling upward* as a writer once wrote. "You mean maybe Pavia's just sick of doing everything right?"

"Fuck up your marriage for no reason, have a kid by yourself. That's a start."

I thought about telling him more about Pavia—her going to the airport to ask the Reeds for money, her recent odd reactions and decisions, her refusal to talk about any of it. But I didn't think Walter wanted to hear it. In any case, I didn't know how to describe it. *Your oldest daughter is becoming weird and remote, repetitive and familiar, like the sound of an ice-cream truck that you always hear but never see turn down your street.*

He didn't want to know and I didn't either. What did I want? I wanted Pavia to stop screwing around and pull it together. I decided that Coach Kessler, quoted in the newspaper in the sports section in front of me on the table, said it best: we needed someone to step up and play that position.

I watched my father smash out the cigarette in the ashtray with his thumb, spit out a few flakes of tobacco that had stuck to his tongue, and fill in 26 and 27 across. I watched the last threads of smoke unravel toward the ceiling and disappear.

"It's strange," I said, "Sometimes it's hard to remember that you ever lived with Dorothy, or with me and Pavia."

"That's why we have written records," said my father, the librarian. He ticked off another crossword clue without looking up. "You still keeping a diary?"

"Not a diary," I said, irritated. Diaries always say MY DIARY on the cover. They have gold-edged pages and cardboard straps and cheap locks with two tiny keys. Diaries are laughable as chastity belts, strictly for girls.

"A *journal*. And no, I don't," I lied.

"Damn," Walter said. He sighed and leaned back, looked at me with his green eye and his brown eye. "What's a seven-letter word for peculiar speech?"

Later on that evening, I called Eli at his house in the big city. It was two hours later there, almost midnight, and I wondered if he would be asleep.

"Hello?" It was a girl's voice, half-laughing, on the line. The phone was passed to Eli.

"We're a little wasted," Eli announced unnecessarily. He meant himself and his roommate, Cassandra. I had never met her; she was a friend from the three semesters he'd spent at art school. I had reasoned she must be sexy in a modern-dancy sort of way; clouded in the smell of essential oils and used to rolling around on the floor.

"What are you doing?" I asked in a high, stenotic voice. "I mean, what are you up to?"

"Well, we're drinking of course. And playing poker. And listening to music. And what else?" Cassandra said something to Eli in the background. "Oh yeah, we're reading personal ads in the *Urban Weekly*."

"Sounds fun," I said. "Who all's there?"

"Nobody. Cassandra. Steig is out of town."

Steig was Cassandra's boyfriend. He was an Israeli painter, a professor at the art school, who had a wife and child back in Tel Aviv. Cassandra modeled for him, and thus hit the whole trifecta: girlfriend, model, muse. Muse sounded like a good job. What were the qualifications, I wondered? Possess an inner fire? Embody feminine mystery? Be beautiful, unusually limber?

"I was just calling to say I made it here." With my tongue, I found the tattered edge of my thumb's cuticle; I gripped it with my front teeth and pulled down hard. "I made it to Supernal. Quite a drive."

"Ouch!" Eli laughed. "Cassie took my chips! She's the biggest cheater. And bitch. A poker bitch. But that's great you made it, Thea. Yeah. "

"Well, I fly back tomorrow," I said quickly. "See you soon."

"Hey—okay. Miss you." His voice got softer as the background music got louder in exactly the way that unimaginative pop songs end by repeating the refrain into infinity as if tagged DNR, Do Not Resuscitate, a recursive decrescendo unto death and the next song.

"Bye." I said, "Miss you," I said quickly and hung up. I had a jaw full of tension and a thumb that was still bleeding when I took it out of my mouth to look at it.

I called Pavia next. There was no answer. The answering machine picked up and I was reminded that it still had the old message on it: Jack's voice, deploying the hale-and-hearty tone he used at work, upbeat about his absence and eager to return my call. So I thought about calling Jack at his new place just to say hi, but I didn't have his number.

I was sitting in the kitchen; in those days Walter didn't have a cordless phone and so I had a chair pulled up next to the phone in the wall. The twisted cord in my lap felt like some kind of diseased body part; a blocked intestine? A varicose vein? A failed umbilicus? Who else could I call?

I heard Walter, asleep, turn over on the couch in the living room. I reached out and pulled a picture frame out of the bookcase next to my chair.

In the frame was a black and white photograph of my parents on their wedding day. In it they are standing next to a three-tiered wedding cake. My mother, her pregnancy hidden under a highwaisted white dress, is young and beautiful with movie-star waves of blond hair gleaming like Cling wrap against her neck. My father is a boy, tall, with shoe-polish hair cut close above his ears. There they were. Dorothy is looking down at her hand on the shiny knife, and Walter is behind her with his hand over hers, helping her push it in. Both my parents are smiling the small, terrified smiles appropriate to real love. On top of the cake, the fat baby Cupid has a cruel grin and a bow, no arrow; evidently his arrow has already flown, struck, pierced, stuck.

As I held the photograph I heard squeaks from the back bedroom, then the sound of Dorothy turning the bedroom door handle the wrong way, then the right way, to open it. She came slowly down the hall and stepped into the light of the kitchen where I was still sitting with the phone cord in my lap and the photograph in my hands. Dorothy's hair was high and flat on one side, smashed into a jaunty, going-to-the-races shape.

"Hello, darling." I was surprised to hear her voice. She smiled gently at me and it hurt sharply, how much she has always loved me, how wrong I'd been to think she would make me return to stay with her in Supernal. "Where's your father?"

I pointed toward the living room, and she nodded. Then she saw the photograph in my hands, and when I started to tuck it back into the bookcase, she moved toward me. I clenched my jaw, characteristically. I thought she was going to want to look at the photograph more closely. I thought she was going to reminisce.

Instead she came and stood next to my chair, leaning against the wall as if we were in a waiting room with restricted seating. She put one smooth and chubby hand on my shoulder.

Perhaps if I had had a terrible illness in childhood—leukemia, cerebral astrocytoma—she would have stood like this and been all right. She would have had to take care of me. I could have drifted off to sleep in her arms, the heart and O2 monitors blinking in the dark like stars, like moons, abiding as rhymes and waves on the sea. *What a wonderful mommy you are, you are, you are! What a beautiful mommy you are.*

Dorothy was stroking my shoulder, then my hair. "What's

the matter?" she asked vaguely.

My throat was tight, hot; I couldn't say. I shook my head. And when Dorothy took her hand away, then my corrosive tears rolled down. They scored shiny lines on my cheeks the way acid rain makes cathedral angels cry even as they smile, because the people who made them and loved them are dead.

15. WHEREVER YOU GO, ONTOLOGY

The self is a corrugated shell, semi-hard and molded to your back, as ugly as expensive luggage. When you travel, it hurts more when you arrive at your destination; it's bent a bit now, dented.

Or else there's no such thing. The past clicks shut behind you like the clear door of a shower stall. You step forward and are suddenly drenched in the future, new as nakedness.

Which is it? The only way to know, my darling, is to go as soon as you get your chance. Go, go, go, and remember me.

The Nile is a river in Egypt, and it flows through the reeds and papyrus, and each second it is renewed. It carries the baby in a basket of grass, into someone else's arms.

16. FOUR MONTHS ON FAST-FORWARD

The next few months in the big city passed with an unnerving steroidal speed. I shall narrate.

Eli met me at the airport the day I got back from Supernal; he had borrowed Pavia's car to come get me.

"How come you're here?" I demanded. He was waiting for me next to a life-size cutout of an Italian papa, who was welcoming us to the big city and in particular, to Little Italy's many fine restaurants for every budget. Eli was mirroring Italian Papa unconsciously, his arms wide open to me, unafraid of new and expanded business.

Eli's ears were still red from the cold and his hair curled a bit over them and he was taller than Papa and so real, and so plainly beautiful, that I was startled. Further, I was slightly offended to feel so quickly disarmed, disqualified, pinned to the mat. After all, I'd been angry with Eli.

"Aren't you too hungover to be here?" I handed him my shoulder bag, which was very heavy.

"Not too much to be here," Eli said, and kissed me.

And so for the time period in question we began to be an actual couple, Eli and I. I finally met his roommate, Cassandra, who was as gorgeous as I'd feared yet surprisingly interested in and nice to me, plus often miserable; I liked her. She loved Steig—who taught at the art school and was hairy and voluble and skeptical-looking, with full, curving lips. When Steig was in the big city he sketched Cassandra over and over again, from every angle, and sold the drawings of her and went back to his family in Israel every six weeks. And when he was gone, Cassandra looked blank and undrawn, pale as paper.

And coincidentally, whenever Steig was gone I tended to break up with Eli, though usually he didn't realize it. During one such time, I had sex with one of the graduate students who moved in two places down from Pavia—he rode the same bus I did every morning, and had read the book I was carrying around, which I never did finish. Another time Cassandra and I went to a rock show together and kissed and stroked each other's arms up and down, but we got tired and gave up and we never got around to it again. It seemed that wronging Eli—even with pre-emptive intentions—was more gratifying to contemplate than to do.

Of course also during this time I was learning about Eli. I learned that he liked to draw on napkins at restaurants, liked to ride his bike, gave careful directions to tourists. I discovered that he phoned his parents twice a week, that he was neat and could fix things. I found out the names of his previous girlfriends—Christine, Anna, and Robin—and that he was still friends with all of them (except Robin, who was crazy), and I observed that men often hit on him, too, because of his prettiness. I learned Eli's smell and how his hand closed to hold mine firmly and automatically when we walked down the street. Naturally, the more I learned about him, the angrier I became. For I believed that he was going to break up with me, and it was hard to forgive him for that. Hence the subtle breakups and mini-wrongings, see above.

I believed that Eli would break up with me the way I had really believed, at least six times previously in my life, that I was pregnant. More than a suspicion, it was a set of unmistakable symptoms. It was a tenderness in my breasts. It was the slight nausea when, for example, a beautiful coffee-shop girl handed Eli's coffee to him over the counter. It was the generally swollen feeling I had, as if—god help me—I were becoming even more excessive in my person, even more needy. It was a metallic taste in my mouth, like a poison, that made me say cruel things to him.

Only in fact, I didn't say them. I rehearsed them in my mind as if in preparation for quick-cut sequence of daytime drama highlights.

>*It must be nice, going through life being so terrific.*
>*Go ahead and sleep with her; you obviously want to, so why prolong the buildup?*
>*You're only with me to make yourself look better by comparison.*
>*You suck at pretending you're not bored.*
>*You're so kind you make me want to stab you with this fork.*
>*For the record, I've had better.*
>*If you knew what I was thinking right now, you'd appreciate my restraint and love me more for it.*

A gallery agreed to have a show of Eli's photography in April, and for two months before the opening he used a copy of the key Steig gave him to get into the art school's darkrooms at night. I used to come along some of the time. I'd sit in the murky room on a stool, agitating, not stirring, the fluid in the trays. Under the plastic tongs I watched the pictures appear on the paper, flimsy and half imaginary-seeming. We listened to The Clash through speakers trashed by sequential semesters of art student use, and we talked.

"Did I tell you about Pavia's baby?" I asked one time. Eli was a dark shape at the sink, edges lit from the blue overhead bulb. "At the ultrasound?"

"Yeah. Boy, right?"

"Right." I made the heartbeat noise under my breath, double-time to *London Calling*. I thought of the little fetus—gelatinous, skeletal—occupying Pavia's middle, moshing in his watery sac.

"What if we had one?" I agitated with the tongs some more.

"Ha." Eli turned to pin a photo up on the line to dry, then faced me again through the murk. "But you're on the pill, you said. "

"I know. Relax." I opened and closed the tongs to ventriloquize the syllables. "Re-lax, E-li. I-am-not-preg-nant-nor-will-I-be-so."

He turned away, wiping his hands on his corduroys. "I am relaxed, Thea. You brought it up, remember?"

"*Suuntsaa*," I said, "Peace," as Eli closed the door of the developing booth behind him as he stepped inside.

The water ran continuously from the hoses, rinsing the prints. I thought of Dorothy, washing and washing her hands in a communal sink at the hospital.

"Thea, do these suck?" His voice was muffled from inside the booth. "I'm looking at all these negs and the prints and I'm thinking...."

The booth buzzed as the developer was switched on. I put myself in an image: I was sitting in the half-dark outside the box that contained my boyfriend, and I was surrounded by his photos—shots of people and plants, pets, toys. Did they suck? As we used to say in those days: *Who knew?* Not one of the photos was of me.

Eli's voice continued. "They're boring. I don't like the darks on a lot of the prints. I'm wishing I had time to shoot a bunch more, but probably I should go with what I have." The buzzers went on and off again. "God. I feel like just dropping off the prints and leaving town before the show even opens."

"You can't do that," I said. "You won't know how it turns out."

Eli opened the door of the booth, and my small, transparent heart was like a minnow when you shine a flashlight on the water at night.

"Eli, they're great. Believe me," I said, and he pushed a hand through his black hair and grimaced gratefully through the murk.

Somewhere along in here, January to April, Dorothy was officially declared Treatment Resistant, which Pavia, Walter, and I were gratified to hear. To us, this was much better than Situational, Likely Responsive With Additional Interventions. No one in our family really wanted to intervene anymore.

Except Pavia, a little. She had the good idea to have herself named our mother's legal guardian. This, Pavia said, was insurance against Dorothy's inevitable next episode. As her guardian, Pavia could prevent her from getting credit cards. She could make sure she didn't, for example, sign a lease on a luxury condo, get addicted to video poker, or invest in a home-based business vending Sealyxyr, The Seaweed Secret to More Passionate Living.

"Now this arrangement still leaves a few things on the table," Pavia pointed out to Walter and me. "Stuff we still won't be able to prevent. Sexual indiscretions, for example."

"Yeah," I said, "And the composition of overlong poems, or the channeling of Claus von Bulow's comatose ex-wife."

"Sunny?" Pavia had asked.

"Sunny."

"The thing is," Walter had said, feigning pragmatism. "It's safer. You can make decisions about her, if you need to." He meant that when Dorothy got too far out there—a dot in the sky, disappearing like a kite snapped free from the line, or when she was free-falling back down, silent as Skylab—Pavia could get her. She could send her to Caldo Springs Center for Mental Health, pronto. Which was where Dorothy was anyway, most of that late winter and early spring. She was receiving inpatient treatment to which, apparently, her brain's receptors were not receptive. Rather, resistant. And when she had finally been released, it was to Pavia's oversight, meaning she (Dorothy) went home alone. Walter saw her twice a week, and Pavia called her every Sunday, and sometimes I got on the phone, too. Things were back to usual, more or less.

"I should start nesting," my sister announced one day in the grocery store, in the household items aisle. She had finally started to read the books about pregnancy that I'd checked out from the library; they were so long overdue she may have decided to keep them. "Getting the house clean, setting up the baby's room."

"The only thing I felt I urgently needed to do was get Dorothy in hand," she continued, eyeing the tub and tile cleaners with a shrewd gleam in her eyes. "And I've done it. I could feather the whole townhouse with paperwork from the lawyers."

"Good insulation."

"Maybe it feels that way for you," my sister said mildly. She gripped the grocery cart handle—revving, revving—then reached for something on the shelf. Overhead, the speakers played a creamy instrumental version of *Ob-La-Di, Ob-La-Da*. I hummed along; *something-something-something in the marketplace, something-something singer in a band*. From the corner of my eye, I was looking at my sister in the navy maternity dress she'd worn to work that day; my sister, balanced like Justice with a jug of bleach in one hand and a bottle of Mr. Clean aloft in the other, reading the label. In that moment I decided that Pavia, who with my help had managed to re-pull things together—including Dorothy, more or less—was going to be all right. She was! And so was the baby, responsibility for whom, I soon learned, Pavia and Jack had decided to share.

"It's co-parenting." Jack explained a few days later at dinner. He rubbed his brow with his knuckles and looked sideways at Pavia, then reached for the salt and pepper. "Shared governance."

This reminded me of how, seven years earlier at a pancake house in Supernal, Jack had announced his and Pavia's wedding plans. "Merger," he'd said then, and he had brought his wide hands together gently, his eyes and eyelashes gummy with unshed tears. Now there I was again in one of life's bigger moments, watching my brother-in-law push food into his mouth with a fork. But this time I sat next to my enlarged sister, feeling the radiating heat of her gestation, understanding—better than Jack would have, certainly—what her obstetrician had meant by the word "effacement." And I felt solid this time, weirdly entitled, the way you do when you watch a young businessman—someone about your age, maybe—trying to catch the bus in which you're riding as it begins to move away from the stop.

This businessman is sprinting in his good shoes through the curb slush. His tie is streaming behind him and his briefcase is banging against his once-muscular thigh. He makes a fist to hit the moving bus; his eyes meet yours through the window glass. The bus driver will stop for him or he won't—but there's nothing you can do. For this you are grateful. You hate to think how eagerly you'd watch the man's face as the bus pulled away from him.

"Baby'll be co-branded, then?" I asked, resting my wrists on the edge of the table. "A nice hyphenated last name? Baby Betwixt-and-between?"

Pavia looked at Jack, who looked back at her uncertainly. Eli kicked me under the table. *What's your problem, pal?* I said turning to Eli, except I didn't actually say anything.

Also in these four months, the baby grew. It went from stapler-length to A4 paper length. Its eyelids creased. Its bones extended towards each other and fused, co-branded.

In these four months, Pavia became the sort of pregnant woman with the high, round belly—the sort who also packs well for work trips, of which there were several during the time period under discussion. Her belly pushed out the front of her work blazers like a sleek accessory, ergonomic, something on which she could rest her wrists during presentations to briefly ease the slight weight of her laser pointer. She was still working very hard.

And her hair was growing longer and thicker; it was growing darker and more shiny. "Don't let me do it. Don't let me get the Mommy haircut," she told me repeatedly, "A big body with a tiny head...a human dollop. No." Pavia was letting her hair grow and grow. And when she let it fall down around her shoulders or tucked it behind one ear as she read the morning newspaper and her cheek showed—smooth as a child's, pink from sleep and 45% increased blood volume—she was more beautiful than ever.

"She's a Madonna," Cassandra said after she met her the first time. "She's gorgeous. And, you know, she's got that calm vibe." She nodded, gathering conviction. "I mean, the Virgin's always so serene, so clear." Cassandra slowly spread her hands on either side of her own midsection. "She's always like, 'Behold.'"

I beamed at her. "You think?" Pavia did seem more settled, if incurious, lately. But that was a good thing, a quiet taking-care-of-business thing. The old Pavia.

At that moment, Cassandra and I were walking away from the apartment, and I turned around and gestured back toward it. "Behold!" I said, pointing to its blank front window. "Behold!" I said, pointing to Pavia's parked car.

"Behold," Cassandra said significantly, reaching over to yank the lapel of my jacket. "Because seriously, there's no way you could afford that nice a place on your own."

"I wouldn't even have a job without her."

"Can she find me a job?" Cassandra worked part-time for a phone sex company. "Can she find me a better boyfriend?"

"Maybe," I said. "She might be all done with hers, by the way."

Cassandra sighed and buried her chin into the collar of her second-hand fur. "The thing is, I'm not done with mine."

Also in these four months, I accepted a collect phone call from a jail in Montana; Joseph was being held for writing bad checks.

"Yeah, jail. It's okay," he said. "Keeps me from drinking." He sighed, cleared his throat. He apologized for not having more news; the trouble was, he explained, nothing much ever happened in jail.

"Nothing happens—if you're lucky!" He gave his high, light laugh. "And how are you folks? How's Pavia's papoose?"

He wanted to be reminded of the due date and the sex of the baby. He asked about Jack and Eli, and about my job. He asked what books I was reading. The prison library had a lot of Louis L'Amour, apparently.

"And your mom?"

I told him that she had been in the Corda Springs mental hospital, and that we had arranged for Pavia to be her guardian.

"That's a great idea! People are always going to want to take advantage of her, you know."

"I know."

"Nice lady," he said.

"I know."

"She wasn't always like that, Thea."

"People always thought she was nice."

"No, I mean she wasn't always so *out there*. Like now. In her own little world, you know?"

"You think?" I asked. "How would you know?"

"When you and Pavia were little, she wasn't so bad."

"She wasn't so good, either."

"Hey," Joseph said firmly. "Look at you and your sister."

"Who, us? The people without a TV?"

There was silence on the line for a minute. "You need a TV? She loved you, Thea."

"It was a 27-inch, practically brand new," I said. Of course, by then Pavia had bought a new TV, but Joseph didn't need to know that.

He sighed noisily into the receiver. "Well, I'm on your dime, so I'll let you go."

"Okay."

"Give your mother my love."

"Ick, Joseph."

"Hey, what?"

"Ick you and her."

"We never did it, Thea."

"No?"

"Wasn't me," Joseph said, "No way. She's like a mother to me."

"Well," I said, "Good luck with that. And good luck with the rest of your jail time."

"Thanks," Joseph said, and hung up.

I put the phone in its cradle and thought about calling Dorothy then. I could tell her that I had heard from Joseph and that he had asked about her. I could ask her if she had had any boyfriends we didn't know about, and if she'd been tested for STDs. I could let her know how Pavia was doing and tell her that I missed her. But before I was done thinking of things I could say to my mother—things I should say—I had forgotten all about it and four months had passed.

17. MORE ON UGLINESS

Clinical studies have shown that sleeplessness clouds ethical decision-making. Do I sleep well? Am I tired? My moral compass is a pinwheel.

In those days in the big city, Pavia's next-door neighbor Calvin—tan and flamboyant at forty-eight, a former Southerner discovered one day (by his mother, Tookie) in his teens having sex with the (male) gardener, forced to leave his home and inheritance carrying nothing but a seersucker suit and a tapestry of cranes highstepping among Medieval reeds—took care of a Haitian woman who lived down the street from us. She was dying of AIDS. Three times a week, Calvin brought the woman dinner. He washed her sheets and bleached them, ironed them. He chatted with her in French and rubbed lotion on her feet. He brought her flowers from his front garden—or else he bought them at the corner florists—and put them in a vase on a chair next to her bed.

Pavia introduced me to Calvin on the street one day. He was wearing white slacks, pulling a picnic basket out of the trunk of his vintage roadster. He was on his way to the Haitian woman's house.

"Her name is Fleur," he told Pavia and me. "Isn't that a pretty name?"

Calvin was movie-star handsome, tall and broad-shouldered; his polite attention to me was almost painful. I opened my mouth and said the food looked nice; he was nice to bring it.

Calvin looked at me then, narrowing his blue eyes a little. "Nice?" He smiled, and my heart spun in my chest like a flower on a thin stem in the wind. He reached out for my forearm and pressed it as if checking for substance. "Well, it's not nice. It's simply not *ugly*. There's never any need to act *ugly*."

Then he was striding away from us down the street, the picnic basket hooked over his elbow. The red soles of his buck shoes turned up in a rolling visual rhythm as he walked away from us, *whoosh, whoosh, whoosh, whoosh*.

As you beat your way into the world, my girl, remember what he said.

18. THE EVENTUAL NURSE

The radio was on in the kitchen and Pavia was pouring herself a cup of coffee. She was wearing a black skirt suit with a blazer that tied in a bow in the back; a Potemkin suit, all business up front and femininity behind. I had just come into the kitchen bringing the newspaper off the front steps when she let out a small, terrified laugh and put her coffee cup down. She peered down at her drenched nylons and shoes. The amniotic sac had broken like a water balloon dropped from a fraternity house balcony.

The floor—I thought immediately—the floor should have been mopped more recently. Why hadn't Pavia mopped it? Didn't she care? Fluid gleamed on the floor.

"I'll call a taxi," I said, "And Jack's work." Pavia went upstairs to change clothes and get her bag for the hospital. I called the taxi and then Pavia's office and my office. I called Jack and left a message.

When Pavia came back down the stairs she was wearing a t-shirt and sweatpants pulled up as far as her thighs. She was holding a rolled towel between her knees and was pressing it against her crotch with both hands, reaching down around her belly. She shuffled toward me.

"Not sure," she said, as if I'd asked a question. "I'm still leaking. Leaking like a...what?" She stopped, feeling something uterine or just trying to recall the idiom. After a moment she continued to slide her way forward toward the couch in the front bay window. From there, she could watch for the taxi.

"Like a sieve," she said.

I ran upstairs to change clothes. Eli had left his Cramps concert t-shirt in a loose, Eli-smelling ball on the floor, so I put that on, and black jeans. As I came downstairs again I could hear General in the kitchen, lapping up the amniotic fluid with a faint galloping sound.

"Ah," Pavia was saying in the front room. I found her with one knee up on the couch armrest, humping it a little, unpleasantly.

"Don't I look like I'm in Drama Club in this outfit?" I asked, pushing down on her shoulders with both hands.

"Prop master." She stared at me. "Lighting designer?" She took a deep breath in and let it out.

"I thought labor was supposed to start out slow," she said in a low voice. "This is fast. Is it supposed to be happening this fast?"

"You were born fast, according to Dorothy. She thought you were going to be born in the car. " I scanned the street for the taxi. I jostled her shoulder a bit. The street was full of morning traffic, and incredibly not one of the sedans, trucks, station wagons, coupes, or delivery vans was a yellow taxi stopping at the curb in front of our townhouse.

General padded into the living room, licking what must be (it came to me) his *chops*. We lavished our divided attention on him; his long, unbobbed tail—an extension of the spine, as Pavia had once pointed out—whipping the side of the couch. I willed the taxi to appear in the window.

"It's fast. It's fast," Pavia was saying again in a minute, shutting her eyes and lowering her head god-fearingly.

"You know what's weird?" I had just spotted the taxi, and I grabbed her duffle bag, then put it down again when I saw Pavia's face. I put both hands on her hips and pushed down as I had seen demonstrated in the *Illustrated Guide to Labor Coaching: 200 Ways to Support and Sustain*. I nodded wildly at the taxi driver, whom I hoped could see me in the window.

"You know what?" I said again to Pavia, grinning insanely through the window, "You've been saying it's fast for the whole nine months."

And then Pavia was through the contraction, and I grabbed her bag again and my backpack. I saw her bending down again to stroke General's furrowed brow once, twice, thrice....

"Pavia. Taxi. Let's move it!" I yelled, and I pulled open the door.

And outside in the big city, spring was apparently happening just at that exact moment. The low morning light flashed in our eyes, the new air rushed into our lungs, and all the city birds hanging in all the branches and dark wires and lines and lamps and signs were suddenly tweeting and warbling like groupies, like conventioneers, like Moonies at a mass wedding—cheering us, selling us, hoping for us keenly with full-throated, reedy song.

When Dorothy was twenty-three and pregnant with her second child, she wanted things to be different this time around. With her first baby, she had been afraid. She hadn't known what to expect. The pregnancy was accidental, and then the baby had come so fast, and then when she arrived it had been so much more difficult than she'd thought it would be. Plus, she (Dorothy) had gotten sick!—and then her mother had come to stay. And it was like when you're carrying something that's too heavy, and so you hand it to someone to hold so you can make an adjustment—get a better grip, fix the weight balance—but then they won't give it back. Alva never gave Pavia back.

It was like: *I said you could borrow it, not have it!* Pavia and Thea used to say that to each other all the time, later, as little girls, tugging from two sides.

So as her belly grew with the second baby, Dorothy reminded herself that this baby would be hers, truly, to deliver naturally and breastfeed and imprint upon and bond with. She pictured it emerging from her body like the second Russian doll inside the biggest Russian doll, shiny with phospholipid lacquer and plumped by good prenatal care, pre-molded to her, fitting.

Dorothy can remember what she hoped for so much better than what actually happened. For Dorothy the hoped-for version is always more real.

What actually happened was that her doctor told her to come to the hospital on a Monday. So she and Walter came together—Alva stayed with Pavia at home—and they stood at the high reception desk and filled out the papers.

"Good luck," Walter said, and then they led Dorothy away down the hall and put her in a room. She changed into a gown, and they started an IV. They left her alone with a copy of *Ladies Home Journal.* And the labor pain did begin more slowly this time, but of course it grew; it changed form. It was hurting, and then it began to pull her apart. Dorothy pushed the button on the side of the bedrail because she believed she was being destroyed. *Can this marriage be saved?* She thought about what she had hoped for—getting through labor as a whole woman, a grownup, a real mother—and realized that there was no use.

The nurse took a long time to come. Meanwhile there was just the bed and the sheets, and the IV tubing and bag on the metal pole. If the nurse ever came, she could take an inventory. She would find all of these objects—metal bed, white sheets, tubing, bag, pole—intact; and on the floor and on the trays and in the corners of room the nurse would also find a thigh, a hip, a throat. These would be the various pieces of Dorothy's body of course— gray, bloodless, drained by a solid, disassembling pain....

"This is labor!" the eventual nurse said. She laughed a little as she said this, in the way that people term *not unkindly*. She gave Dorothy some gas to breathe in through a mask, and then left her alone again. And when she was gone, the labor continued, the same except now at a great, uncrossable distance, until it was the next day. And then Dorothy found herself in a different room, and a baby in a wheeled bin was parked next to her bed, its forehead dented by forceps and its small mouth moving like one raised disk of a tentacle.

Meanwhile, in the hospital waiting room, Walter smoked and watched television. Along with another man and the man's mother and mother in-law, he watched a cooking show and two soap operas.

"It's baby number one for us," the other man said, leaning forward on his seat and clapping his hands together like a quarterback waiting for the snap. He was about Walter's age, wearing a dress shirt and nice slacks, his brown hair oiled and raked across his scalp. He looked familiar; he might have been in Walter's Basic Chemistry class at the U. "Your first?" the man asked.

Walter nodded, then shook his head. The mother and mother-in-law exchanged glances, alert to potential tragedy. Had he lost his first child? He noticed that the women sat next to each other, not on either side of the man; they were friends. Together, they were going to become grandmothers.

Walter's own mother had died in his freshman year of college; she had never met his wife or his mother-in-law, or his baby, the first one. Walter found himself actually telling this to the man and the man's mother and mother-in-law.

"I'm sorry for your loss," the man said, and rubbed his chin stubble. He sat back in his chair again and moved his eyes to the television. But the grandmothers had found each other's hands, and the one with curly hair was looking at Walter gently.

"She's here in spirit, though, your mother," she said, and Walter nodded. Then he looked away too. He felt in his breast pocket for his cigarette and matches, and pulled the ashtray stand closer to his chair.

Where do they get the white sand for these ashtrays anyway? He tried to imagine a place in the world where the sand could be so pure, so fine, so soft. Where you could walk through the sand barefoot and your feet—hairy, waxy, yellowed from years in socks and shoes—would become coated with tiny flakes of mica. The mica would sparkle with each step and protect you, and you could walk forever without tenderness like a god striding across the sharp black sky.

Walter's mother had been quiet. Unlike Walter's father—or, Jesus Christ, his own mother-in-law, *Alva*—she hadn't told Walter what to do at all. When the mimeographed list of academic courses had come in the mail, one day in the summer before college began, they had sat at the table together and looked at it. She had worn the black reading glasses that she kept on a loop of string around her neck.

One by one, Walter had pointed out the classes he was thinking of taking. "That does sound interesting," his mother would say, and she would circle each description with a pen. She had sat next to him and she was as tall as he was, and her hands were long and her fingernails rimmed with dirt from the garden.

She had smelled faintly of sun and Jergen's lotion. And she was going to die within two months and leave Walter behind, and if he had known this at the time, then everything he remembered later there in the hospital waiting room would be retitled *The Last Days of Her Life*, like some stupid soap opera, so it was good—it was good!—that he didn't.

Pavia and I arrived at the hospital, and after Pavia signed in we were led to a delivery room. "She wants an epidural," I said to the nurse as I watched my sister changing into her hospital gown; it was touching how awkwardly my sister moved, lifting each foot out of her sweatpants with the sad, dutiful concentration of a circus elephant climbing down off the overturned barrels.

Weeks before I had asked Pavia how she was imagining her baby's birth. She had eschewed the Prepared Childbirth classes advertised at her OB's (and recommended by me). But was she going to do some special breathing? Visualization? Was she going to have a natural birth?

"Natural? You mean, like, with no makeup?" She had smiled at me. "No. I'll do whatever it takes to feel as little as possible."

But at the hospital, pain relief seemed not to be a priority for the staff. "She wants an epidural," I said again, this time to the nurse who took Pavia's blood pressure and slid a monitor across her belly. And eventually a third nurse brought in a clipboard of papers to sign; when they were complete, she told us, they would page the anesthesiologist.

Pavia was sitting in bed by now, her arms crossed over the draped berm of her bosom, her eyes closed.

"Sign these," I said. "Sign these to get your drugs."

She opened her eyes. She shook her head.

"I've changed my mind. I can do this without the shot."

The whites of her eyes were scribbled with tiny blood vessels—a movie screen showing the hairs stuck in the projector. I held the clipboard and felt the seconds race past us with a fearful, whirring sound. Why was my sister letting that pain go on; why wouldn't she take something?

"Sign them in case you change your mind," the nurse told Pavia mildly. "Then we'll have them all ready." Pavia unfolded the pale arm she had clutched around her chest and gently pushed the clipboard away. Dismayed, I handed it over and the nurse left the room.

"Okay," I said, leaning into my sister, who had dropped her head and was now rocking back and forth. I put my hands on her back and pushed in. "Tell me why no drugs," I said when she had straightened up again. "This is awful, Pavia!"

"This is labor." Pavia let out a frayed breath. "It's supposed to hurt."

"Why?" I sounded like a child.

"So when it's over, you won't be the same."

I hated her; I nodded. "But I want you to be the same."

She reached for the giant cup of water on her bedstand and drank through the straw. She pulled her hair off her neck and reached to me; I pulled off one of the hairbands around my wrist and gave it to her. "And I have chapstick." I dug into my backpack and brandished a tube.

"Great. Keep it up. Soon I'm going to be pretty useless, you know. And you're going to have to help me."

"No. No, no, no. You can do it," I said as I watched her use the chapstick, my own lips stretched wide in sympathy. She handed back the tube and looked at me, waiting for the next contraction. I saw my last best chance.

"You could be the same after this, if you wanted to." I whined slightly, I'm afraid. My sister looked past me, up to the place where the beige curtain around the bed hung from little plastic beads to a track in the ceiling. She was listening, perhaps. "But you've already been changing, Pavia."

"I know," Pavia whispered. She knew I wasn't talking about the changes to her body. She lifted her hips up off the mattress, slowly pulled the hospital gown down around her thighs. "I know. Before you came I wanted to shake things up. Now, I can't stop. You know? Like a beat?" She patted the sheets. *Thump thump thump.* "I wake up in the morning and I try to keep things straight, but I don't know what I'm going to think about anything. About Jack, or this baby or the other one...." *Thump. Thump. Thump.* And then the next wave came.

Pavia buried her face in her hands. The bedside monitor dragged its needles across the paper, tracing the contractions and the baby's heart rate. It wove each tracing into the lines of the graph paper like Penelope killing time waiting for Ulysses. The used paper curled off the end of the machine and fell to the floor in a long, drooping loop; a regular epic.

"I bet that's how Mom feels most of the time," I said as I watched the top line on the monitor climb higher toward the peak of the contraction.

"God, don't say that," Pavia said in a muffled voice. Then she started humming into the pain, her voice buzzing in her hands, the theme from *Bewitched.*

Hours later that day, finally, I climbed into bed with my sister and knelt behind her. I leaned into her and the heat of her body came into me, and the pain pressed back as a slab.

There was a nurse named Ellen with us during this part; she was holding Pavia's hand. And when Pavia finally began to cry Ellen stepped back looking fierce, as if she herself had had enough. With vengeful-seeming dispatch Ellen turned from the bed and snapped a latex glove on her right hand. How we loved Ellen for that!—because then she gripped Pavia's knee with the ungloved hand and went in with the other, her mouth making a hard circle as her fingers blindly climbed toward Pavia's cervix.

"You're there," Ellen reported to us, "Ten centimeters. Almost time to start pushing." Ellen left to summon the doctor, tossing the glove in the wastebasket by the door on her way out.

The doctor—not Pavia's regular doctor but the guy on call, young and athletic looking—came in smiling. He pulled the wheeled stool to the end of the bed and sat down, getting comfortable. He reminded me of the ferrier at the interpretive farm that Eli and I had visited on a recent Saturday—all hot irons and broad grins, holding forth about Keeping This Traditional Craft Alive as he hammered gaily away and drops of molten metal seared black pocks into the tops of his boots. With comparable relish, the doctor flipped his tie back over his shoulder and bent between Pavia's trembling thighs.

"Perfect ten!" he confirmed, and motioned for the birthing bar to be fitted to the bed. This was a U-shaped bar that fit upside down—the opposite of a lucky horseshoe I couldn't help noting, which must be hung with the open part up, lest all the good fortune drain out—into two holes near the end of the bed. We helped Pavia grab onto the bar and squat beneath it. The doctor started to explain how to push but Pavia was already at it. Ellen was at her side talking in her ear and I was propping her from behind on the bed, and then eventually Jack was in the room, too. I had forgotten about him. The shape of his body displaced some air as it moved across the tile floor toward our bed....

So Jack held the cup of water then, and Jack spoke into Pavia's ear. Jack became the one who counted to ten during the contractions, tearing off each small piece of time for Pavia as she bore down desperately and then rested in between. He had the part where he says to her each time, "All right, let's go again. One, two, three, four...."

Pavia would look at Jack wearily, maybe trustingly. She would close her eyes again. And I lifted my sister toward her husband as she fought in ten-second bursts to get out of the way of that baby, who was coming, who was coming, who was coming down like something hammered from above, something driving through and splitting her open.

Then the doctor was telling her the baby's head was crowning. Pavia clung to the bar and drew in her breath for one last push. I was leaning into my sister, lifting her up—and I felt the baby leave her body all at once. Jack yelled "Oh!" as fluid rained down on the linoleum at the end of the bed. And my sister's back was heaving like she couldn't breathe and I was thinking *put it back! put it back!* until I heard that hackneyed newborn cry and Pavia—with the sound of bellows opening up wide—took a filling breath between my hands at last.

I looked over my sister's shoulder. Ellen was lifting the baby up in two gloved hands, the little culprit. Covered in blood and smeared white and yellow with vernix, the baby was moving, undeniable, raw and unprocessed. Suddenly wild-eyed, it jerked and swiped a tiny red fist at the doctor, whose name none of us remembers now.

The doctor clamped the umbilical cord and invited Jack to cut it. "Feels like cutting a fruit rollup!" Jack sobbed to no one in particular, and handed back the scissors, handles first.

Thus my nephew was born on April 10, 1994. His mother and his father named him Xavier Alva, and we all upticked one notch toward death—Pavia, as usual, a step or two ahead of me.

19. ON THE APOCALYPSE

In college in Supernal we had a nuclear clock. I don't mean an atomic clock; this was a painted clock, red, on a sign outside the Humanities building. The short hand was always on twelve and the long hand was always some minutes just before twelve. The clock was counting the seconds until nuclear midnight, when all the world would be ablated, aborted, abjured.

We had seen the simulations, how one missile—or one erroneous report of same—would trigger a retaliatory missile, and back and forth etc. until the warheads crisscrossed in the air, canceling each other like two typed keys—first the letter X and then the backspace key—taking stupid turns. Thus, according to the model, the world would be destroyed ten times over.

Now you'd maybe say, *you wish*. You wish it would be that sudden and complete, or that you could imagine the world times ten (even negated)—ten perfectly punched holes in the vellum of the galaxy. Because now the data are in and we know: the apocalypse happens slowly and is never quite complete. It's global warming and polluted water and genetically modified weeds. It's drug-resistant strains of this and that, more gated communities, more glue-sniffing street kids, more people who want to have a baby but can't because of endocrine-disrupting plastics. Worst of all, it's the knowledge that this world is the only one we have, ours to ruin just once out of negligence and a feeling that we have more time.

I'm sorry that this is your time, my darling, and that we no longer have a clock to check ourselves against. Still, I'm here. And I'll stay beside you for as long as I can.

20. LIGHT POLLUTION IN THE NEWBORN PERIOD

After Xavier's birth, Pavia developed a case of postpartum pre-eclampsia and needed to stay in the hospital for four days. Jack stayed too, in a little nest of flannel blankets he had made in the bedside armchair. Sitting there with X tucked against his left forearm and bicep—and greeting each visitor with a look of proud expectation—he inadvertently created an awkwardness that limited visitors to a few short minutes each.

"Aren't they...separated?" asked Pavia's assistant, Kathleen, in the hallway. She hugged a teddy bear to her chest protectively when she spied Jack through the window of the door.

"Hey. Nice to see you," Eli said, glancing uncertainly at me.

"Weird," Cassandra commented on her way out. "But whatever."

In the bed next to her husband and son, Pavia seemed to ride on an unsteady cushion of narcotics and edema. "My vagina is down by my knees," she said as she climbed back in bed after a trip to the bathroom. She touched her swollen face with her swollen fingers. "My face fills the room." The nurses materialized every few hours to help her with breastfeeding, kneading her and X together in various positions. Pavia pursed her lips above her newly doubled chin, breathing carefully.

"I don't think he's hungry," Pavia would say skeptically, which is to say she mused. "Look, he's still asleep. Anyway, I don't have my milk in yet."

Nevertheless the nurses—lactation consultants, Jack seemed gratified to hear them refer to themselves—continued their relentless ministrations. And on the third day, in accordance with their assurances, Pavia's milk rose up. Moored at her chest, her breasts filled and lifted like two miraculous pontoons, white and worthy. Thus encouraged, X began to feed better, clinging to them with his sharp-fingered little hands.

Of course, during this time in the hospital Pavia's bedside phone rang again and again. Whenever I answered I told people that Pavia was resting comfortably. This sounded like a nice thing to be doing, and Pavia didn't want to talk anyway. She wanted to sleep.

Eli took a photo of her that way, Pavia asleep with her hair ratted up behind her on the pillow like a dark mantilla, her puffy hand across her chest showing pink where they had had to cut her wedding ring off the day before. He took a picture of X, too, while the co-parent Jack held him up in front of his own face and smiled broadly and irrelevantly behind the wall of X's curving newborn back.

And so it went until breastfeeding was well established and the patient's (Pavia's) hypertension had resolved, and it was time for my sister and X to go home. Jack and I packed up, working side-by-side like a pair of sister-wives. Over the last few days the room had filled up with instruction sheets (*Vaccinations, Signs of Jaundice, Precautions Against Infant Abduction*), stuffed animals (bunnies, lambs), and personal hygiene products (Maxi pads, Tucks, barrettes). We took everything, threw everything into plastic grocery bags. We agreed to leave the flowers on the windowsill; the nurse told us that the flowers would be given to patients who didn't have any.

"Second-hand flowers?" Pavia asked as she walked reluctantly over the threshold, looking back into the room.

"Keep going," I said behind her. I was carrying a duffle bag and the car seat, and Jack was right behind me holding another two bags. The nurse was last in line, pushing the baby in the wheeled bassinet.

At the nurses station they checked Pavia's wristband against X's before letting us sign out. They handed Pavia her sawed-off wedding band in a Ziploc bag. Jack tried to slip a baby sling over Pavia's head; she blocked him with an upraised forearm.

"Batik." Pavia said.

I shook my head at my brother-in-law, but he began to talk anyway. "My parents brought it back from Jamaica. This is how they—"

"No." Pavia lifted X from the bassinet and began fitting him into the car seat. She glanced at the wad of colorful fabric in Jack's hands. "No."

The nurse looked at Jack and shrugged. She watched Pavia fasten the rigging of the car seat tight around the baby. Then she checked it—it was tight enough—nodded, and bade us goodbye in a satisfying, chapter-ending way: "Drive carefully now."

And off we went, Pavia first with the car seat, slowly, then Jack, then me—three grownups shuffling down the glaring hall with our miscellaneous burdens banging quietly against our knees.

"Do you want me to carry that?" Jack caught up to Pavia. "Him? The baby?"

"Jesus Christ," Pavia murmured absently. "Who wants second-hand flowers?"

Of course, just as the closing of a door signals the opening of a window, the end of one chapter is also the beginning of another. And as forecast, things were different once we brought X home.

For one thing, the lighting was different: Pavia couldn't stand having the overhead lights on, and she kept all the curtains drawn. Only a few small lamps lit the apartment. In transit between sleep and wakefulness, between feedings, diaper changes, and X's surprisingly forceful eruptions of spitup, my sister padded around in the new, picturesque murk. In the circle of Flemish light below each table lamp there was a still-life of apple cores, folded sections of last week's newspaper, and baby bottles with curdled breastmilk clinging to the sides. My sister's thinning face was half in shadow, Pavia the Elder....

Outside, excluded, spring continued to develop. "This time is going so fast," Jack would remark to Pavia. He was coming over after work each day and staying the night so he could help with the middle-of-the-night feedings. Each evening the supposedly estranged couple would share a beer sitting side by side on the couch, X balanced on Jack's wide thighs. With all the attention and tenderness of a bomb squad, Pavia and Jack would unwrap X from his blanket and begin to catalogue his components.

For example, the new co-parents noted that X's eyes were large and gray and were likely to turn hazel like his mother's; he had his mother's sidelong, appraising gaze, too. His thin arms were like Jack's, already lumped with shoulder muscles. X's hair was entirely his own and surprisingly self-contradictory, curly in the back but straight on top, black over the fontanel but pale white— almost fiber-optical—at his ears and neck. Most amazing of all, it seemed, was that their baby knew them! When Jack reached for him and called his name—*Xavier!*—their baby lurched from semi-consciousness and waved his spastic limbs. Also (I noted) the dog trotted in from the other room.

"It's a reflex," I told them, breathing through my mouth; they all smelled faintly of vomit. "This move"—I flung my arms out in an ugly way, clawed the air—"is the Moro reflex. He thinks he might be falling."

"Nah." Jack shook his head and fit his finger inside X's little fist. "He knows his mom and dad. And she doesn't get it, does she Xavier?" Jack asked the baby, whose eyes rolled up inside his head, then found their way down again.

"That's okay," Pavia whispered. She kissed the top of X's head. "That's okay."

Jack looked at his watch, and Pavia absently squeezed one breast, then the other. "Time to nurse," Jack crooned, and bent his head, too, toward X.

I went to get the breast pump parts that were drying in the kitchen sink—no one could say that I wasn't helping!—marveling anew at the apparatus: two clear plastic funnels, two tubes, two bottles to collect the milk. It was hard to believe that technology hadn't evolved past this. *Milk, milk, lemonade—round the corner, chocolate's made.* You attached all the parts to the grinding motor—encased in a doctor's bag of wipeable faux leather—and fed the breasts into it. In relentless bursts of suction the nipples were pulled to twice their usual length. Milk sprayed out and was collected; the infant was fed. The breast pump was a horrible analog for maternal care—brutish, mechanical, too straightforward—and naturally I was fascinated by it.

Pavia's technique was to nurse X on one side while pumping the other breast. His weak little chin bobbed fiercely beneath the breast he was latched on to, syncopating the sound of the pump's motor.

"Listen," Pavia said, nodding at Jack. "Bar-ry White, Bar-ry White, Bar-ry White. That's what the pump sounds like."

"Hmm." Jack smiled, inclined his head toward his wife. "Or fis-cal year, fis-cal year, fis-cal year. No, wait. It's Uruguay, Uruguay, Uruguay." He smoothed the fine black hairs over X's forehead with one finger. "Should we go there someday, Pavia? Uruguay?"

Pavia looked down at the bounty gathered around her chest—infant, apparatus, familiar hand of estranged husband— and smiled like the Sun Maid raisin girl with her harvest tray.

"Maybe," she said. She sighed and closed her eyes; she chanted, "Barry White, Barry White, Barry White."

Each morning during this newborn period, I left similar dimly lit, affectionate, and confusing scenes, and each evening I returned to them. Calling Pavia from work I would picture her still sitting on the couch where I'd last seen her, waving to me as breastmilk wet the front of her t-shirt and tears streamed slowly down her cheeks: "No, we're fine! Jack is here! All we need is more orange juice!" The townhouse was a fluid underworld, with Jack always there like a shadow across the surface, and I felt by contrast grotesquely solid and concrete, heavy.

I was now the main dog-walker in the family, and as I trudged behind General each morning in the stink of early spring— yards and parks full of thawing trash and unidentified organica—I cultivated a list of grievances and regrets. I worked on the list the way other people run the lint roller over their clothes before going to work, or pat their pockets to check for their keys, or wash their hands over and over again, or count the steps in every staircase they descend. It was part of my daily hygiene.

Jack is taking advantage of Pavia during a vulnerable time.
She should have divorced him, cleanly and finally, while she had the chance.
While I had the chance, I should have joined the Peace

Corps.

I could join the Peace Corps now. I'd become a stronger and more generous person—not to mention more focused —plus people would miss me a lot.

The fact that I dread talking to people I don't know well forever precludes my success in investigative journalism, human rights activism, and documentary filmmaking. Being self-centered is also an obstacle.

I am like my mother, extravagantly unequipped for life in the first or third world.

Pavia's love for X is also extravagant. It's excessive. It's overparenting as a distraction device, X being the fulcrum of her and Jack's seesaw codependency. Or not, because what would I know about excessive love?

In any case, it's clear: Jack is taking advantage of Pavia. She may seem okay now, but as she used to say Grandma Alva used to say whenever she (Pavia) was laughing too hard: "It'll end in tears."

It will end in tears, I somberly thought to myself, walking along behind General in the park, mud sucking at the bottom of my shoes. The dog paused and crouched; I stopped too, waiting for his shit to fall, my outstretched hand clammy inside the plastic bag. In my mind, then, I heard again X's first astonished, raspy cry as he slipped out of Pavia's body and landed, wet and warm, in our world.

In that early newborn time, part of the problem was that Eli, too, was leaving me behind. He had had his show at the gallery, and he sold some photos ("pieces"), and he'd been invited to be in another group show with people I understood to be very cool.

By way of illustration, here's an image (a "piece") from that second gallery opening: Eli with one hand in his pocket, the other holding the plastic cup of white wine, nodding happily as a petite woman—a woman perfectly and slightly miniaturized, as if Xeroxed at 85%—talks softly in his ear. She's rocking forward in her kitten-heeled boots as she talks, both hands curled around her cup. She has huge black eyes and red lips, soft-looking white hair curving like a serif around her dark throat and shoulder. She's wearing a black wool dress buttoned in front from her neck to her ankles. One bump in front is her breasts, one bump in back is her ass—she's balanced there like a typesetter's dream, an unusual ampersand come to life.

Next: Cassandra and Steig, postcoitally entwined and pleased with the universe, slouching arm and arm across the gallery floor toward Eli. Greetings and hugs—Steig and Cassandra know the Ampersand, too, it seems—and everyone is smiling. Eli now has both hands around his wine glass as if to center himself.

I was standing with Pavia and X nearby this scene; it was one of X's first outings. Pavia had him in a little pouch—not the batik sling, but a black affair that pressed him to her chest almost punitively—and she was spearing cheese cubes with a toothpick, one after another, and pushing them into her mouth as in an automated process. I was wearing a black canvas skirt, flat Mary Janes, a rumpled green cardigan with a t-shirt underneath.

"Try to look more like a breeder, would you?" I suggested to Pavia. "Maybe get Xavier to cry? Maybe you could nurse him while you stand here eating?"

"I could really Mommy it up, if you like," Pavia agreed vaguely. She looked over at Eli's group. "People would think you're the nanny. The hairy German nanny."

The Ampersand laughed in a silvery way—or in a way reminiscent of some other soft metal, aluminum or nickel—and Eli gazed at her with a slack look of appreciation.

"She's not his type," Pavia said under her breath. She

leaned over the table and palmed a short stack of sesame crackers. "Anyway. Have you actually looked at any of the photos yet? Let's check them out."

So my sister and I did a circuit around the gallery, standing in silence before each print with the heightened awareness (mine, not Pavia's) that the young men standing next to us (a.) were moving along the gallery's perimeter in the opposite direction from us and (b.) each weighed less than Pavia and I, individually. With their narrow hips and bony wrists, their heavy glasses, their dirty hair gelled up in signifying ways, they were serious and architectural. They made Eli seem robust by comparison. They were a type of young man not available back home in Supernal.

And the girls at this event—the young women? Perhaps you can imagine. I could hardly stand to look at them and I still don't want to think about it.

Pavia fed crackers into her mouth as we moved along; occasionally X's shape squirmed against her torso before settling again.

"Hey Thea," she eventuated, "Aren't you in any of these photos?"

I shook my head. "It's not a Cassie-and-Steig kind of thing," I told her. "I'm not Eli's *muse*."

Pavia chewed; cracker crumbs drifted down onto her son's head. "Well, what are you then?"

We were looking at a photograph of a kid in an Orange Crush t-shirt, standing with his mother by a token machine in the subway. The child was looking cross-eyed up at the camera and giving the finger. There was a yellow dot sticker next to the card on the wall; someone had bought the photo.

"I don't know what I am. Maybe I'm Eli's habit? Not in a chemically dependent sort of way, but more in the way of a routine. An activity of daily living. Like brushing your teeth."

"Okay. Brushing your teeth." Pavia moved to the next photo, continuing her straight-ahead stare. "But what if Eli loses interest...meets a Water Pik or something?"

I felt my neck fatten and warm familiarly; it was embarrassment or woundedness or mild sister-hatred, maybe all of the above.

"Or if he starts to floss...?" She continued, rubbing X through the fabric of the sling.

"Shut up," I said to my older sister. Pavia clucked at me, kissed X's head once, twice. "The thing is," I said, looking reluctantly around the room, "I do like these pictures."

Pavia nodded and put her arm around me; in the harness between us X hung like a heavy ball. "So do I. Maybe we can get one for Xavier's bedroom."

"He doesn't have a room. I'm in it, remember?" I took a cracker from Pavia's hand and fed it into my mouth, took a gulp of wine. "So what about Jack, anyway? Are you guys getting back together?"

She shook her head, shrugged.

"This will be confusing to him, you know," I went on, pointing at X, her son. "And really, do you think you're being fair to Jack?"

From across the room came another laugh from the irrepressible Ampersand; I didn't need to look over to know it was her. Eli and Cassandra and Steig were yucking it up as well. In Pavia's ear I continued. "I know the extra help is nice right now, and I know you want Jack involved."

"It's not just involvement."

"Co-parenting. Still. There are no boundaries. You've got no plan. You're playing house again, and..." I had stopped because I couldn't think of my next line, and the pause was swelling now into inadvertent significance—"and it's messy. And it's mean."

"How so?" Now Pavia's neck and cheeks were brightening, too. I was pleased to see this. "How is it mean?"

"Jack assumes you're going to reconcile. He can't help but think that—he's over every night. Don't you think that's kind of cruel?" I realized I was a little drunk; my own voice clamored flatly in my ears. I took a breath and went on.

"I mean, don't you think it's kind of cruel to just roll along like that? And Xavier..." By then Pavia was looking at me two-dimensionally, like a photo of a person saying *I dare you to go on* or like the image in the rear-view mirror of the animal you just failed to miss running over.

"Xavier won't understand. Are mommy and daddy together? Are they not? Is this what a healthy relationship looks like? Is this a functional dynamic?"

Pavia pulled her free hand through her hair and pointed her eyes at me. "Like you would know."

"I know the opposite." I bent my arm around her waist and squeezed, incidentally just as my eyes met the Ampersand's. She (my sister) shrugged out of my single parenthesis and turned to face me.

My dark-haired sister was staring at me, her baby strapped like an X of bullets across her chest. *I can't really hurt her*, I told myself. *She has everything!*

"What is it then?" Pavia asked. "What do you want, anyway?"

I looked at my sister and bitterly I mused. *Everything.*

I took a falsely ragged inward breath. "I just don't want you or Xavier to get hurt," I said, passing off a look of understanding.

Pavia watched me for a moment, then turned away. I followed her. We went from one photograph to another on the wall.

"Or hurt Jack," Pavia said at last, quietly. She hiked X up an inch by cinching down on the strap.

"Or Jack," I said approvingly and with a kind of cold relief. I gulped my wine until it was gone. "Is it time to feed Xavier?"

Pavia reached under the harness and copped a feel of her breasts. She nodded. I looked over at Eli's klatch; over the Ampersand's creamy head he caught my eye and waved. I motioned toward the door and mouthed goodbye, re-looping my arm around Pavia and her child. Unfashionably conjoined and definitely downbeat, my sister and I made our way through the gallery toward the door and out it.

It was a warm evening and the city was just starting to throw a dome of light pollution into the air above us. The early stars were shoved away. We sat on a park bench across the street from the gallery. Pavia nursed X for a few minutes while I watched people come and go across the street, the music gagging repeatedly as the gallery door opened and shut.

When she was done nursing, I put the harness on and put X in it and we headed toward the subway station. Later, as we rode on the train, X's head moved around on its little stem as I held him against me. Next to me Pavia had her arms crossed in front of her, looking at the dirty floor of the subway car. When people got on at each new stop—an Indian lady in a sari and sweater, an elegant older couple, the usual furtive kook in an army jacket—they each glanced at us and assumed that the baby was mine. They figured that *I* was the good and attentive mother and that Pavia was self-absorbed and unhelpful, the irresponsible one.

At least that's what I remember assuming others were assuming. That night is not so clear for me now. It was a long time ago, before there were other, more surprising, signs about what I was and Pavia could become.

21. YOU WON'T KNOW ME

Of my formal education—K through 12, plus a bachelor's in communication—there are artifacts, and they are like things in a curiosity shop.

The location and chief products of Dahomey, a West African kingdom that no longer existed by the time I glossed its encyclopedia entry for my third-grade report.

A description from *The Martian Chronicles*: "Delicately sensing decay at last, the regiments of mice hummed out as softly as blowngray leaves in an electrical wind."

The accounts of certain women in the Middle Ages, whose ecstatic religious experiences included marrying Jesus using his snipped-off foreskin as a wedding ring.

My point is: who knows what you'll remember? And of what you remember, how much is true?

My point is: you won't know me. You'll be tempted to think you do—I have mastered my mother, haven't I, in the neatest possible way?—but darling, no. You won't know me.

I was a person before you were conceived, and inside, your mother is (I am) as weird as love, as lonely as a survivor, as gone from you as a vanished nation. I was there for you, but inside the disfiguring crust of motherhood. Not so you'd know it.

22. THE REPUBLICAN

Three months in from X's birth, and it was full-on summer. On the days Eli worked in my building, he and I were eating lunch outdoors, suffused in a chlorine mist as we sat on the edge of a sponsored fountain in the corporate plaza. At home, Pavia turned on the cooling units in the windows during the day. Also, she had started calling in to her office. She had found a daycare for X and was going back to work.

And although I told myself I was not directly responsible for this development, Jack's visits had titrated downward. He and Pavia had had a talk that Jack summarized one day on the front steps as he was leaving, pink-faced and brave, one arm in his windbreaker, thus: *We need to achieve greater clarity around our relationship, and refocus on our shared goals for Xavier.* For the moment, that was going to mean a more strictly divided style of co-parenting. Tuesday and Thursday and Saturday evenings Jack would tend X without Pavia.

"It's a good thing I taught Xavier to take a bottle," Jack had grimly declared that day on the steps. I nodded. He had managed to get his other arm in the windbreaker, and now he clapped his dry-looking hands together like chalkboard erasers.

"Want to get a drink?" I surprised myself by saying suddenly. I nodded toward the corner, around which there was an Irish bar, The Republican.

Jack nodded, and I pivoted on the steps and went back down the street with my brother-in-law. As we walked, our afternoon shadows crossed and recrossed ahead of us on the mottled sidewalk.

"You guys had such a huge wedding party," I began brightly, shifting my backpack to the other shoulder. "What was it, ten bridesmaids and ten groomsmen?"

"It was a big group. Fraternity brothers. Man, I don't even know where most of those guys are now."

"It was eight years ago."

"Eight years." Jack reached up to touch a branch of the tree we were walking under. "That was a good day."

"Yeah. Remember Dorothy's dress, though?"

Jack smiled a little and shook his head.

"And Dad put his cigarette out in the wineglass? And then what's-her-name drank from it?" Now Jack laughed. "See? We are a fun, fun family," I said, pushing open the door to the bar and holding it wide for Jack to go in first.

Inside The Republican it was cool and dark; I noted with gratitude the absence of Irish music playing on the sound system, music that by the second beer always begins to sound like the soundtrack to my own personal horror film—all frantic jigging and reeling, the heroine threatened by tight-smiled, high-stepped earthiness.

Jack and I sat down in a booth and ordered beers. "Yes, you and Pavia have a really fun family," he said, a little warily. "So what's next?"

I looked at Jack. He was thirty-one but he looked older—

maybe forty-two or so—but then, he had always looked forty-two. He probably would look forty-two until he died and my guess was that it (his demise) would be due to something cardiovascular. Jack was tall and wide, sandy-haired, with big, tubular arms and the expression of contented mischief that long-approved-of boys tend to have. I supposed it came from self-esteem. Yet there he was, one of life's winners, sitting in a bar with me, a long-faced girl with glasses who was biting her nails. What would his fraternity brothers say if they could see him now?

"It's hard to say what will happen," I began. Our beers arrived in front of us on the table, and I took a long, stalling drink.

"You sound exactly like Pavia."

"Genetic, I guess." I sucked on my ring finger, which had begun to bleed as a result of my pulling the cuticle off with my teeth. "Anyway, what does Pavia say?"

"You probably know more than I do. I mean, *I* don't know. We're just...we're all about Xavier, and we're together all the time, and so to me it feels...it feels like a good fit." Jack bridged his fingers together in front of him on the table. *Here's the church*, I thought.

"Maybe she doesn't want to be fitted, you know?"

Jack shook his head.

"Maybe she's changed—maybe she needs some room."

"Did she say that?"

I shrugged. Hoisted eyebrows briefly.

Jack took a judicious breath in. "She communicated to me that she thinks we need to be somewhat conservative as we determine our next course of action as a couple. With Xavier. I mean, as a family." He folded his hands together. *Here's the steeple,* said his index fingers, or maybe it said *POW!*—as it was gun-shaped, too, that two-handed church.

Jack shook his head slightly, looked up at me. "That's not the same thing as needing room, is it?"

"Boundaries, space...." I weighed my beer in the air against my empty hand.

Jack sat back in the booth. The bottom lids of his pale eyes sparkled suddenly with heavy-looking, unshed tears. I waited; he blinked. Tears fell.

"I've never understood what the fuck this separation was all about in the first place," he said. "Fuck." He wiped his face with a wadded up napkin.

I put my beer down and placed my palms flat on the table like a seer. "Neither have I, Jack." I shivered inwardly at the weird intimacy of saying his name.

He reached over to my hand, squeezed it. "What should I do?"

His hand on mine was like the image on a sympathy card.

"You should keep your expectations low," I told him. This was fair advice for all of life, I quickly reasoned with myself, fair play. "And be there for Xavier, of course."

The Irish music started up on the speakers overhead after all.

"Tuesdays, Thursdays, and Saturdays," Jack said bitterly, raising his voice over the music. "Others by appointment, I guess."

Jack was still gripping my hand; I squeezed back hard. "She does want you there," I said.

He shook his head. "Last summer she asks me to leave, so I do. Then I find out she's pregnant, we're still talking all the time, seeing each other, she has the baby." He rapped my knuckles on the table for emphasis. "She has Xavier." It's clear he still can't believe it, even after three months: he's a father. "My little baby."

"My little baby," I repeated softly for some reason.

"Uruguay."

"Pavia's always said that it was me." His eyes flickered over mine. "That I'm the dad." The statement curled up between us like a fallen question mark, a hook at the end. Jack let go of my hand.

"Yeah, she has."

The door to the bar kept opening with a squeak, then banging shut. A sign behind the bar said *LADY'S DRINK FREE ON WEDNESDAY!* I thought: in a world full of misplaced apostrophes, you might as well let people make their own mistakes. So I waited and waited, not looking at Jack or saying anything more while he considered his paternity and his wife. He was moving his plastic cup around on the table as if searching for the right spot for it, and he was likely arriving at the wrong conclusion—about Pavia, I mean, not the cup—and I offered him no help or reassurance.

"And I should keep my expectations low?" His chin jutted out as he looked down at the table.

I kept on saying nothing. He laughed in a small, joyless way that slightly offended me: that was *my* laugh he was using.

"What expectations?" he suddenly answered himself. "I don't know what the hell Pavia's doing. I doubt she does, either."

Under the table, my toes tapped involuntarily due to Irish music and the need to pee. Also anxiety. "But like you say, it's been ten months of separation," I finally said. "Not so much clarity yet."

"I have a clear schedule with him—with Xavier. But no fucking idea where our marriage is heading."

"Strategies, but no vision," I said sagely, squeezing in the sides of my plastic cup. "That's hard."

He looked at me then with a kind of fullness, and I imagined what it would be like to kiss him. And then suddenly that's what I was actually doing—half-standing, leaning over the table,

155

buttressing myself with my knuckles. Our lips pressed against our teeth and softened only a little, at the end.

I sat back down heavily on my side of the booth. The music jigged and reeled—*magically delicious!*—overhead. And thank god my brother-in-law didn't say anything or look particularly moved as he sat across from me. I'd known him for eight years, and we'd never really understood each other, though holidays and special events with alcohol had tended to reveal a surprising sort of love.

The person who loves my sister.

The person who loves my nephew.

The man with the briefcase, running to catch the bus that's pulling away.

I do love him, I said to myself in a childish and deliberate way. "Love you," I apologized to Jack.

"That's what they all say." Jack sighed and stood up, hitching his khaki pants up by the belt; he seemed to have lost weight. He reached in his back pocket for his wallet and put a five on the table. "See you later, Thea."

"Tuesday night."

"Right," said Jack, and walked out the door of The Republican. I poured the rest of his beer into my cup; I put my feet up on his side of the booth to signal *no company for me right now, thanks.* Not that I was in any danger of getting hit on: the small red proto-pimples on my forehead were shiny and probably catching the light from the Bud Light sign topographically, plus my hair was lank and two loops of sweat hung in the armpits of my blue cotton blouse. I was, in a word, *premenstrual*, which is to say once again I was still unpregnant, a loser in love.

X's daycare was in the same industrial park where Pavia worked, in the building next to hers. "So that's good," she would say, as if continuing a commentary. There was no extra commute to get him there, plus she could see him at lunchtime. And it was convenient for Jack, too, who still worked at Pavia's company, but in another division.

"So that's good," she would add.

On Tuesdays and Thursdays, Jack picked X up and brought him back to the house. Jack fed and bathed him, talking softly to him, coaxingly, half-fearfully now as if to a voodoo doll. X—chubbier now, more vigorous, more Jack-like—gurgled back or farted softly through the fabric of his onesie or clutched a small handful of his father's face flesh and was unable to let go, and his father would laugh. Pavia would sometimes ask me how these evenings had gone, and I reported them faithfully (see above).

She would nod vaguely at me. "So that's good," she would say again.

"What do you do, anyway, when Jack is tending Xavier?" I asked Pavia once while she stood at the kitchen sink washing out parts of the breast pump. Per their agreement, she was staying away from the house on the nights that Jack watched X, coming home in time for one last feeding before bedtime.

"Errands. Grocery shopping. Dry cleaning," she said. "Sometimes drinks with the girls." I had no idea who the girls might be; maybe her assistant? All her life, Pavia had had boyfriends, not real friends. She had never seemed to need them.

Pavia had rinsed out the clear tubes that came with the pump, and now she whipped them around her head to centrifuge out the drops of water still inside them. She was like Wonder Woman with her lasso, dark-haired and chesty, a superheroically grim expression on her face as she determinedly whirred. Suddenly something struck me.

"Jesus Christ, watch out!" I slapped my hand over my cheek, leaned away from her and her tubes. She was tense, my sister—keyed-up, avid. The postpartum transition back to work is a difficult passage for many working women, as is marital ambiguity—I knew this; nevertheless, naturally, I blamed her.

"I can't believe it. You just whipped me!" My cheek felt hot and shameful, rebuked, Biblical. Already I could feel the rising line of the tube-shaped welt. I started to cry.

Pavia yanked open the refrigerator door and reached into the freezer compartment. She held out a blue ice pack and stared at me as solidly as a blue ice pack.

"Sorry."

When I didn't take the ice from her or stop crying after a moment—in fact, I was genuinely having trouble stopping the crying—she slammed it down on the counter, flung the tubes next to the espresso machine, and walked out of the kitchen.

I recognized that I was being a baby, going on and on like that. But my cheek hurt. My boyfriend wasn't adequately attentive. My uterus was out of order. And something was starting to go wrong with Pavia, and that certainly wasn't good. You may remember: it happened to Dorothy.

Dorothy, back at home in Supernal and on a regimen of polypharmaceutical checks and balances by that time, was up again. Walter stopped by her house every day on his way to work to make sure she was taking her medication, and he gave us the report.

"What can I tell you?" he said over the phone, irritated. "Let's just say she's really fucking busy."

"Busy," I repeated from my seat in the front window of the townhouse. It must have been a Tuesday or Thursday because Jack was there with Xavier. "Busy doing what?"

"She's writing another book."

"On Jackie Onassis?"

"Do you think I ask? Anyway, her thing is all cleared up, I

guess."

Her thing. The pause that ensued should have been awkward. Walter was talking about Dorothy's sexually transmitted disease, which they'd discovered at the mental hospital. This disease, at least, had responded to treatment.

"Should I *clap*?" I asked my father.

"You should shut up," my father said.

"Right." Across the room Jack pointed to X, his own left eye, his breast pocket—he was miming to me that I should watch X while he (Jack) went to heat up a bottle of breastmilk. I gave him the thumbs up.

"So what else is new?" I asked. "How's work?" My nephew was sitting propped up by a donut-shaped pillow on the floor, chewing on a plastic toy phone. Slowly, sensuously, two strands of glittering spittle descended, connecting his mouth to the floor; he ran his fat hands through them the way a harpist rakes *glissando*. X was getting his first tooth, Jack claimed.

"This weekend, I had to cover in the children's section," Walter said, and started coughing. "That was Saturday. Fun."

"How could Judith do that to you?" Judith, the head librarian at Supernal Public Library, was still his supervisor thirty years after she'd hired him. I'd seen her over New Year's; she still had the same head of hair in a flip, body by Jack LaLanne in a washable pantsuit. She and Walter still had coffee every day at ten thirty. They sat in the 3Bee's café next to the library, often each with a small stack of books to trade to the other; they were both fast readers and could each finish several books within the three-week checkout period. Sitting there in the café, they were like one of those long-distance trucking couples. She could have sewn curtains for the sleeping compartment on the cab. She would have chosen a literary CB handle for them—Dashiell and Lillian—and read aloud to him book after book as they sat twelve feet up in the air, barreling along the high plains, Judith's mouth moving soundlessly behind the window glass.

"Budget cuts," Walter said. "It's not like we have a lot of extra staff, and Judith was sick."

"She okay now?"

"Eh," he said.

"She's not gonna die, is she?" X was staring at me, his legs spread wide as he sat ramrod straight atop the fat fulcrum of his diaper.

"Everybody's gonna die. And Judith"—another coughing fit—"just has the flu."

"Oh. Good." Jack came back in the room with a warm bottle for X, who eyed it lustily as it came ever nearer, his bottom gums awash in the tide of incoming spit. "But anyway, you think I should call Mom?"

"If you want," Walter said. "She might be too busy, but yeah. That'd be nice. Call your mother. And tell Pavia...tell her that for a visit, I'm thinking about the fall. Give a kiss to the baby. Now goodbye." He hung up without waiting for me to say goodbye.

"Dad says they're thinking of coming to visit in the fall," I told Jack, who was feeding X in his (Jack's) lap. "Both he and Dorothy."

"I can't believe he can wait that long," Jack remarked without looking up, "He hasn't even seen Xavier yet."

"Well that's the point, isn't it?" I said irritably. "He's coming to see him. He doesn't know what he's missing yet." I looked at Jack in his knit shirt and Chinos. *At least our parents don't wear matching sweatsuits*, I wanted to say, though this was only half true I remembered with a pang. So with an inner flounce, I turned away from my estranged brother-in-law and his co-child, and I dialed my mother's phone number.

"Hello!" she answered breathlessly. "Oh, darling, it's wonderful to hear from you."

The window—a real one, not metaphorical—was open; I looked out through the dirty screen onto the street. The light was draining as the sun dropped behind the roofs across the street. A small breeze brought in the smell of the ocean. A couple walked with bare arms around each other, hands tucked into each other's waistbands. They were probably headed for the rock club down the street, where the beer and the loud music and their complementary good looks were going to fill them with what is termed *a sense of youthful possibility*.

"Can I tell you what I'm at work on?" Dorothy started to laugh, her voice carbonated with self-affection. "But to tell you the truth, I hardly know where to begin."

"Me neither." I waved down at Pavia, who had now appeared on the street below carrying two shoulder bags (laptop, breast pump) and a string-handled shopping bag. She was marching forward with a brave-seeming gait, her head up and eyes fixed, no doubt, on our lighted window as her hand brushed against the top of the fence, counting, counting. For her I waved my arm higher, in a wider arc, perhaps wildly, *here we are!*, as Dorothy's voice spilled on and on.

23. IMPORTANT LIFE SKILLS

Cardiopulmonary resuscitation. The Heimlich maneuver.

Outdoor skills: How to blow your nose without tissue. (Lean over, put your finger over one nostril, blow hard—HARD—out the other.) How far to lean back when peeing on the ground, so as to avoid peeing on the back of your pants. (Hug a tree if necessary and possible.)

Additional skills: Parallel parking. Changing a baby. Microsoft Word shortcut keys.

White lies: you're happy to see them; you think they look great; you know they'll do well. Also: you're busy at work; you understand their frustration; you can't complain. It couldn't happen to a nicer person. You're sad to have to miss it.

How to resist the delusion that you are naturally nice and many of your motives are selfless.

How to tie the plastic bag around the garbage can so that it doesn't slip off and fall inside when it gets full.

How to whistle. How to wiggle your ears. How to do a cartwheel, the Hustle, the Macarena.

How to read. How to swim.

How to know when someone loves you, and how to love them back. What to do next. And after that.

24. A SOMETIMES COLORFUL IDEA

Two weeks after I kissed Jack on the mouth, Pavia called me at work. She was talking from the supply closet at her own workplace where she was pumping breastmilk, and so in the background *Uruguay/Barry White.*

"Jack has a girlfriend," she said quickly. For a week or more, from her office window, Pavia had seen Jack doing the half-mile, bark-chip Fitness Loop with a woman.

"She's young and pretty. They laugh. I don't know her; I think she's got to be from Marketing."

"Marketing," I repeated ominously.

"I know. They started off, you know, power walking. But today…" Pavia stopped, shifted the receiver, came back on the line. "Today, they were doing all the fitness challenge stuff."

"She can do a pull up?" Station 5 had a high bar, I knew. At other stations on the Loop: a balance beam, a berm of half-buried tires (agility), slanted tables for situps (core strength). There were signs with hints on healthy eating, calculations for target heart rates, and a treatise on the importance of weight-bearing exercise to bone health. Yes, from my ten days of temp work at the company the previous fall, I knew that Fitness Loop. It slinked around the campus of buildings owned by Pavia's company; it was so varied and relentlessly specific in its suggestions—each fully illustrated and importantly titled, e.g., the Chest Dip, the Oblique Crunch, the Extended Calf Press-up—it was their corporate Kama Sutra.

"That's just it," Pavia said, her voice small. "He helped her do station 5."

"Lifted her up?"

From the phone came only *Uruguay/Barry White. Uruguay/Barry White. Uruguay/Barry White.*

"That asshole," I said. The gray fabric lining of the walls of my cubicle seemed to reach its tiny polyester fibers toward me in a miniature, static-y panic. "Well, look," I said quickly. "Where are you guys, anyway? I mean, were you thinking—ah—were you thinking divorce?"

Uruguay/Barry White.

"In case you haven't noticed, Thea, I haven't had a lot of time for measured conclusions. I just had a baby." My sister's voice rang with the musical tones of mild hysteria. "You know what I was doing? I was, you know, trying to be fair. Remember fair?"

"I guess," I said.

"So now he's going to file for divorce, and I'm going to be a single mom, and there won't be anyone—anyone—who cares when Xavier sits up by himself or if he…," and she began to cry. "If he can pick up a Cheerio."

"I care," I said, and then with the special emphasis that only doubt can provide, "I really do!"

"Great," Pavia managed to say.

I squeezed the phone between my shoulder and bent head, then turned my computer keyboard over and shook out the food crumbs with punishing vigor. My heart was thudding uncomfortably, but I told myself that there was nothing I could do right now except wait for her to stop crying, which she gradually did.

"I've got to get back to work," she finally said. "Talk later, I guess."

"We'll talk later," I replied. "And hey, good for Xavier," I added before she sniffled goodbye. "The Cheerios thing, I mean."

I hung up the phone, and the little red light on the phone console went off. I saved the document I'd been working on—*Developmental Immunotoxicity*—and shoved my chair back from my desk. It was two in the afternoon, and I could tell I wasn't going to be able to find the right thing to say later to Pavia.

And why was that? Why couldn't I be a comfort? Why did I always feel like something tipped over, poured out? I was like the cardboard canister held by the unsuspecting Morton Salt girl; my contents stung the ground in a granular line behind me.

I stood up and looked over the maze of cubicle walls. Keyboards clattered. A phone rang and someone answered it. I had no idea where to go, but I pulled my backpack off the hook and left my office.

Manifesting little imagination but predictable anxiety, I went over to Eli's house. Cassandra let me in. She was on the phone, working. While keeping up a low, monkish chant of *oh babys* for her client, she managed nevertheless to indicate that she liked my skirt and that I should help myself to coffee; by pointing to the kitchen clock she suggested that Eli would be home in an hour. She gave me a beautiful smile, rolled her eyes, and padded back toward her room. It struck me that she was like a friend.

She was my friend.

I dropped my backpack next to the door and took my shoes off. I thought about the friends I had had before I came to the city, and how these friendships tended to end, according to their type: There were girls who I felt sorry for—dull and irritating girls, many with physical impediments to social success (obesity, buck teeth, corrective lenswear, etc.) whom I eventually dropped, at least in part because they demonstrated a failure to understand that it was *I* who was being kind to *them*. These friends felt fake, auxiliary. On the one hand, they didn't count. On the other hand, I owed them everything. At school I often had no one else to talk to; talking to them, my voice bounced back to me as if off a curved shield.

Type 2 friend: smart girls. These were girls whose busy schedules and life plans and precocious accomplishments had estranged them to me, one by one. Girls who, when they went away to camp or college, said, "I'll write you!" and then really did, neatly and on cute stationery. Girls I tended not to keep in touch with and whose mothers, I suspect, thanked me for this.

The third type of friend? The weird girls whose circumstances tended to remove them from me eventually. These were the girls who wrote notes in encoded messages and were prone to sudden tears. They were the nail biters (or, in high school, nervous smokers) and uninhibited singers with perfect pitch and good memory for lyrics. Girls who had crushes on the oldest men on daytime television, the evil patriarchs and neurosurgeons with their five o'clock shadows and expressive eyebrows. Girls who knew all the wives of King Henry VIII and how they died. Girls who liked secrets, promises, exclusive laws and creeds; girls who suggested you be their blood sister and had actually brought to school the knife to cut you with—and it was not a pocket knife.

I had three friends in this last category. The first one moved away, and the second got pregnant and was sent to live with her father in Seattle. The last one, a college friend from Spokane whom we'll call Vivian, gradually became before my eyes the person huddled over coffee in the dining hall, her hair unwashed and her hands shaking badly. *I told you so*, I was always tempted to say under my breath as I passed her table and failed to greet her.

These were, of course, the friends I loved the most, the weird girls. Yet I felt a sickening relief to lose each one.

So that afternoon at Eli's, listening to her muffled voice urging *Fuck me!* from the next room, I poured myself some coffee and considered Cassandra. Odd, smart, and sometimes pitiable, perhaps she was the living synthesis of the types of girls I had hung out with growing up. Perhaps this meant that at age 26, I, too—in spite of recent challenges—was achieving some kind of personality integration?

That thought cheered me. I stirred milk in my coffee with a spoon, enjoying the quaintness of the gesture. It was something one might do in a cottage, whilst visiting one's friend. I thought to start making toast for both of us. I would put it on a plate, with a tidy pat of butter! And later, I would go home and provide appropriate support to my older sister! Who had a temporary case of the baby blues, and who would be fine!

I was standing at the counter, holding down the toaster handle when Cassandra hung up the phone and came in the kitchen.

"Tough day at the office?" I asked.

"Nah," she laughed. "But busy. And I didn't hear from Neil, which is weird."

Neil was Cassandra's favorite client. He was a soft-spoken man, ostensibly mid-thirties, supposedly in the middle of a long sex-change process—post-hormones, pre-surgery. He called the phone-sex service several times a week on a schedule so he'd get Cassandra, and they'd talk about clothes.

"The last time we talked he wanted to pretend he was a bride. I was helping him get dressed for the ceremony."

"How does that work? I mean, how do you do that over the phone?" I asked.

Cassandra twisted her hair up on the back of her head, then let it fall again against her long smooth neck. "I describe how he washes his hair and his body—lots of shaving, in his case—and I talk about the fragrances of the shampoo and soap. I told him the stockings we'd chosen, and all about his makeup, and all about his dress. His dress was really, really beautiful." Cassandra sighed, looking past me. She pointed. "It had all these tiny pearl buttons up the back."

I looked where she was pointing; threads of black smoke were rising from the toaster. I pulled up the handle.

"Yeah. But you know, schedules change. Things come up." She smiled slowly and disingenuously. "I'm not going to take Neil's silence personally."

I nodded and began scraping the charcoal off the toast with the back of my spoon.

"Hey," Cassandra said suddenly, "How's your beautiful sister and that beautiful baby?"

"Baby's fine," I said. I handed her a piece of worked-over toast.

"Uh oh. What's up with Pavia?"

"Postpartum stuff?" I ventured. "Fatigue? The fact that Jack has a little something on the side?" I surprised myself by using that last scorned euphemism. *A little something on the side*—it was a term someone in Marketing would use.

"That's crazy," Cassandra said soberly. "How did Pavia find out?"

I told her about the Fitness Loop; Cassandra shook her head and shivered. "Ugh," she said.

"What about you and Steig?" I asked. I cupped my palm beneath my chin to catch the toast crumbs. "How are you two doing? How much longer is he here for?"

Cassandra's face clouded. "He's going back to Israel as soon as the semester's over, actually." She looked up at me, swallowed. She began to say something, then startled as the front door burst open and banged shut again, hard.

"That scares the shit out of me every time." She looked over her shoulder toward the foyer. "Your boy's home."

I followed Cassandra to the front of the house holding my coffee cup, feeling sheepish, delinquent. It was the middle of my workday; what was I doing there?

"Look who missed you," Cassandra told Eli. Faithful to a domestic practice that didn't exist in Supernal, so far as I knew, Eli was kicking his sneakers off into the pile of shoes by the door. He looked up, and perhaps he looked pleased—but not ecstatic, not thrilled—to see me there. Perhaps I took this personally. In any case, I smiled simplistically, as if without distress of any kind.

Toast sliding around on the surface of our plates, Eli and I had left Cassandra and gone up the stairs to his room. As usual, it was neat and strangely wholesome-seeming. He had photos—his own, friends', photos from magazines—pinned to one wall; his mattress was on the floor opposite. He had clothes folded and stacked in milk crates, a bucket of All detergent next to the door.

"What's up with Cassie and Steig?" I asked, wiping my crumby hand off on my leg and lowering myself to his bed like an eager analysand.

"Nothing that I know of. Why?" Eli said with his back to me, kneeling to put a CD in his stereo.

"She said he's going back to Israel as soon as the semester's over. But doesn't he usually stay here for a while? Usually, don't they like to go on a trip together, or something?"

"I don't know what they usually do." Eli pulled his camera

bag toward him across the floor and unzipped it. He took a camera body out, set it down on the floor beside him, and reached in again for a little canister of compressed air.

"You don't know?"

"I don't," he said. Eli released a little blast of air into the open back of the camera. "But maybe it has to do with the fact that Steig's wife is pregnant."

"Oh my god. Again?"

"Apparently." Eli closed the camera, put it away in its nest inside the bag, and grabbed another. He frowned down as he popped open the back of the next camera and started shooting air into its corners. "That's what, number three?"

I nodded but he wasn't looking at me.

"Yeah, three," I said. "Does Cassandra know?"

"I don't know. Steig only told me last week."

"Did he tell you not to tell her?"

Eli glanced up at me on his bed, where I was lying on my side with my head on my elbow, slumber-party style. He shook his head.

"What does that mean? 'Huh-uh,' he didn't say not to tell her, or 'huh-uh' he wants you to keep it quiet?"

"Thea, he wouldn't ask me not to tell," he said, pushing a piece of dark hair—what people used to call a *hank*, I think—off his forehead, "Anyway he doesn't need to. Why would I mention Steig's wife's pregnancy to Cassie?"

"She has a right to know," I said peevishly. "Wouldn't you say that it's her business?"

Eli looked at me with an ancient expression—the same face you've seen fused on mummies, woven in tapestries, referred to in diaries, caught on film—it's the Look The Dad Gives The Mom.

"Wouldn't you say," Eli said, "That it's none of *my* business?"

I wouldn't have said that; I never say that. I've never had any idea where this mysterious border—my business, your business—lies. I wander around in the desert, crossing *la frontera* back and forth, abandoned by my coyote and delirious with thirst. *Mi casa es su casa.* I stared at Eli wavering before me as in a mirage—actually, my feelings were hurt and unfortunately, tears were in my eyes—and swallowed.

"And speaking of things that aren't my business," Eli was again moving things around in his camera case, zipping and velcroing all the minutely discriminating compartments, "I've never seen you take a single birth control pill, Thea. We've slept together how many times?"

I shrugged and shook my head; once again that day my heart was jumping under the useless adipose that filled my bra's left cup.

"'Uh-uh,' you don't know how many nights we've spent together, or 'uh-uh' you don't want to admit you lied to me?"

I sat up on the bed and put my hand over my heart. "Did I lie?" I think I really didn't know.

"Apparently, yeah. We discussed it. STDs, birth control—you said you were on the Pill. And then later..." he zipped up the bag and shoved it back against the wall by his stereo, leaned back on his hands and looked at me. "From then, you just didn't really mention it. You let me assume we were covered."

"You never mentioned it, either." *Mi casa es su casa.*

"I know." His gaze was free of content.

"Jack has a girlfriend," I said suddenly. I blinked wetly.

"Not surprised," Eli said. "You think he's just supposed to hang around forever, not knowing whether Pavia will ever take him back again?" He glanced at his clock radio; the next number fell down with a tiny clapping sound. "Look, I didn't know you were coming over and I told Steig I could shoot some of his

paintings tonight for a grant he's applying for. So I've got to go."
He stood up, and I scrambled up after him.

His camera bag over his shoulder, Eli paused before pulling
open the bedroom door. "Don't say anything to Cassie."

"I won't," I said to his back, queued up as I was behind him.
He had on the soft blue Indiana State sweatshirt I liked; I wanted
to put my head against it.

I followed him downstairs and out the front door, and we
walked a block without saying anything. At the corner where we
would go different directions—me to the subway, him to catch a
bus—Eli pulled on my shoulder and gave me a kiss on the cheek.

"Let's take a break for a while," he said gently into my ear.
"All right?" I pulled back to look at him, and there he still was,
beautiful and not unkind, not unfair or mine. The sky moved
around in the background behind his fine head. What could I do?
I nodded.

"That'd be good." I smiled to show that I could. I felt like a
skull, my long teeth stuck into dry bone.

"Good. Just some time to think. And I have a lot of shit to
get done this week."

I nodded again. I shaded my eyes to look at his face. I
looked, cleared my throat.

"Eli, just so you know, I've never used birth control with
anyone. And I've never been pregnant. I'm perfectly...I'm perfectly
safe."

He didn't look reassured. "Huh," he said, looking down the
street away from me. "So you say this to all the guys."

I didn't know whether to nod or shake my head; I pulled my
shoulders up in a torticolic spasm, I'm afraid.

"There's my bus." And Eli grabbed the strap of the bag
across his shoulder and took off running like a kid.

And still it was Wednesday, just the middle of the week, and only approaching dinnertime at that. After Eli left me at the corner, I drop-footed my way down the dirty steps at the subway station.

The train was crowded, but I got a seat next to a large lady who wheezed softy as she worked a find-a-word puzzle, persistently missing CREATURE on the diagonal starting top right. On the other side of me, a guy about my age—asymmetrical hair, torn sneakers—had his Walkman headphones hanging around his neck, tinny alt-rock music flowing out soothingly as if on a balmy wind. I could see my way across the subway car to my own reflection in the window as we lurched along in the dark. The gritty glamour of one's image in a big city window has always worked for me, I'm embarrassed to say. Anonymous and advertorialized—I can tell you now that it's the treatment of self I like best, the only one that moves me.

Pavia was sitting on the front stoop when I got home; she must have left work early, too. She held X on her knees, facing out, and he was responding to the early evening stimuli—sun in the trees, smells in the air, car sounds of the after-work commute on a moderately busy street—with a looped series of gags and sighs. General was sitting beside them, head up and sniffing regally.

I slid my backpack off and lowered myself down on the steps beside Pavia. "How are you doing?"

"Better and worse." She kissed the back of X's head on the slot-shaped patch of scalp, the place where the hair gets rubbed off. "Worse because I can start to imagine how it feels, to be really on my own."

She kissed X's head again on the same spot.

"Better because it's always just me, anyway. You know what I mean?" She turned her head and looked at me squarely. "You do," she said finally, diagnostically. "You're alone anyway, in the end. I mean, everybody is."

She looked away, and jounced X up and down on her knees. From the side, Pavia and X had the same eyelashes, the same cheeks and lips; they were two sides of the same coin, new currency from a land of fertility. *At least you have each other*, I thought self-pityingly, but didn't say...she didn't know that Eli had just broken up with me, so there was no way to say that aloud without sounding like I was trying to console her.

Instead I gave her the patented family offering: a look of understanding.

"I know what you mean," I said. "We're all alone." The music from the kid next to me on the subway came back to me as if still carried on that warm, bad-fruit-smelling air that pushes up from the train tunnels. I knew the lyrics. *The sound of their breath fades with the light.*

And it was an austere and emphatic moment—only a little frightening—that I shared with my sister, who kissed again the vacant patch on the back of X's head.

The gray-blue light from the TV in the next room shifted across his arms and shoulders, across his hands. Walter was sitting at the kitchen table, smoking. A book was open flat in front of him. He was having trouble concentrating.

Ha ha ha! roared the laugh track. Walter turned his head to listen; he didn't hear his daughters laugh along in the living room. Maybe the laugh track made it seem unnecessary to have their own enjoyment also audible.

Entering behind him, Dorothy crossed into the kitchen with a trembling glass in her hand. She got some ice cubes from the freezer, then filled the glass at the tap. She moved past Walter again on her way back down the hall to the bedroom. Across his left hand on the open book, the TV light moved like something striking poses.

Hahahahaha! The helpless mirth went on and on, professionally long-lasting. Walter closed his eyes. Now he could pick out the voices of the individual laughers. The man with the deep, contagious chortle. The shrieking woman. The high giggler. He pictured them with their heads thrown back and eyes closed, mouths wide, arms thrown across each other's shoulders, sagging with the weight of hilarity, unraveling because of it....

LAUGHTER, Walter thought. That's what the giant cue cards held up to the studio audience would say. APPLAUSE!

Laughter. Applause. A show, Walter thought, as he listened for his daughters' voices threading through the noise, it's just a show. And soon it will be over, he wished, and then finally quiet.

It was a weeknight. Pavia asked me to babysit on the coming Friday night, and I agreed right away.

"He and I'll cuddle up on the couch and watch a movie, go for a walk," I told Pavia.

"Okay." She looked at me doubtfully. "But Xavier goes to bed at 7:30. Not much time, really."

"Well, whatever. Just the walk, then." I was grateful to have a little job, a little distraction. I had just told Pavia that Eli and I were "taking a little break."

"Never mind," she'd said. "You and Eli? That's not over yet." But her frown as she said this—long-distance and philosophical-seeming, not strictly sympathetic—had made it feel even more final. Not little, not self-limiting.

So after work on Friday I hurried to Pavia back at the apartment. She was waiting for me, standing at the top of the stairs leading to the front door. She had already unfolded and latched the stroller and packed its various pockets with X's surprising array of personal effects—diapers, bottle, toys, clothing. She had X set on her hip; her eyes were bright. She began talking at me as

I climbed toward her, a Slinky of words uncoiling down the steps to meet me.

"Instructions are typed up and on the counter. Bedtime's 7:30—you know that—and he can have a little bottle soon and another, bigger one before he goes down. Sun's still up, so I've got sunscreen on him. Hat," she said, pointing to the mesh bag underneath the stroller seat, "and a bag of breadcrumbs for the ducks. You're going to the park, right? Feed the ducks?"

I nodded. She took my backpack and moved X over to me. She opened the front door behind her.

"Bye," she said stiffly. "You can go now. I just need to get a few things done inside before I go out. I'll be gone by the time you come back."

She leaned in and pushed her head against us both. She kissed X's neck rolls and cheeks, craned to kiss the back of his head. Once. Twice. She breathed his hair, kissed it. Three times. Four. He grabbed a few strands of her hair, which pulled off in his hand as she straightened.

"Ouch," said my sister. "Goodbye. Have fun. See you later." She carried the stroller down the steps to the sidewalk then bounded back up them, General tripping at her heels. She waved at me over her shoulder as she went back through the door. I watched her slender white hand flutter at General's collar as the door closed.

Above the tops of the buildings, the sky was orange though not as in a Western; it was a dirty taffy color. To match, the air was sweet and unhealthy, pre-breathed by the tunnels and manholes and vents, by the five million other residents of the city. I put X in the stroller, unlocked the wheels, and started off down the street. It occurred to me that I could go down the block, see what band was playing at the Arrow that night. Maybe later, when my babysitting gig was up, I'd go to a show. I could stand directly in front of the speakers, blast the self-pitying thoughts from my head. I could go home drunk and with my ears ringing. I'd sleep heavily and dream non-whimsically, if at all.

As I pushed the stroller I didn't think about Pavia. Instead I fixed my thoughts on my uniqueness. I was certainly the only person that sociable Eli Greathouse had expressed an express desire not to see. To take a break from. And if I had known then what would happen later that evening, I would have hated myself even more acutely and specifically for several other reasons besides.

"Later," my sister had said to me as the door was swinging shut, and I hadn't said a thing in reply.

25. OCCAM'S RAZOR VS. THE SWORD OF DAMOCLES

As part of your total colonoscopy experience, you are usually given a drug, midazolam, brand name Versed. The drug keeps you relaxed during the procedure. It also makes you forget nearly everything about the procedure afterwards. With Versed you likely won't remember having the doctor snake your bowels with a 36-inch scope. You won't remember the subtle tugging as your doctor snips off polyps the way a gardener deadheads dahlias. You may only faintly recall (as did my co-worker, Flint) cheerfully telling the story of a hoped-for trip to Glacier National Park, where mountain lions do indeed pose a threat to children and to women of smaller stature. After your colonoscopy with Versed, you feel tender toward yourself in a way that is pleasantly free of context.

Today approximately five hundred thousand Americans claim that they have been abducted by space aliens once or repeatedly. A typical scenario includes a rural setting, a lonely road, the flash of light, the ascent to the hovering ship, and medical procedures *often including anal probing* (italics mine).

You see where I'm going with this: the theory that many of these alien abductions are the by-products—the waste matter or aftermath, if you will—of the use of midazolam.

I believe in theories. Especially compelling and convincing are the ones where a terrible possibility is explained by another unpleasant, perhaps even slightly more painful second possibility.

For example, it's not necessarily that there is no Santa, but rather that everyone has been lying to you about their belief in same. Similarly, it's not that there is no God, but rather that there are many forces making our world, each one idiosyncratic, incompletely powerful, perfectly godless.

As another example, it's not that no one you love has ever loved you back. Rather, it's that the person you love has finally come to know you well enough to stop.

26. THE REVERSE THIEF

To this point in our story, as you may have noticed, several things had prevented me from giving full attention to my nephew, X. Let us examine this lack of materteral attention and its causes.

First, there was the fact that in that period of early infancy Pavia and Jack were always there—always at the house together, bent over X like a pair of tensor lamps. He occupied them physically; babies, as you know, require constant manipulation. But it was a spiritual preoccupation, too. For Jack, this expressed itself as a repeating incredulity, as a sequence of moments of regenerating awe. "Xavier reached for his mobile!" "Xavier looked out the window!" "Xavier smiled at me!" Jack would breathe out heavily as he spoke, like someone noticing that it's raining even though the sun is out, light-filled beads of water falling all around him as in a shampoo commercial minus the sexual overtones.

For Pavia, the spiritual impulse manifested in rituals. Checking twice to see if the door was locked. Waiting till the fourth ring to pick up the phone. Kissing her son an even number of times in the same place, back of his head. All her movements were formalized and careful, sacramental-seeming.

And in response or by comparison I was small and shiftless. I was the acolyte standing to the side; I held the tarnished candlesnuffer. Threads of black smoke rose around me, a sinner....

A second barrier to entry vis a vis a relationship with my nephew was the perceived (by me) fragility of him (X). My backpack—which typically holds my coin purse, my glasses case and repair kit, a book, chapsticks, a bottle of ibuprofen, a bottle of water, a complimentary motel sewing kit, and a sedimentary layer of half-damp and crumpled ATM receipts—weighs more than my nephew at five months of age. And as with my backpack, I was acutely aware of X's location at all times, lest it/he be stolen. This awareness—simultaneously acute and chronic—was a burden to me. Despite what I had written in my QmedCare employment application, I never welcomed additional responsibility.

Further, it was a burden to feel uncared for by comparison to X. It was dismaying how this feeling stretched back toward the baby that was me sitting in my playpen and squinting—as I must have done, as my myopia wasn't diagnosed until I entered kindergarten—at a fuzzy TV screen while Dorothy napped. And now that same feeling stretched forward as well, toward my future self. I pictured myself as an old woman alone, clinging to a radiator for warmth and friendly sound effects.

"Do you wish he was yours?" Cassandra had whispered to me at the hospital the day after X was born. I had looked at her—model, mistress, muse. *A muse,* I thought then, *I finally get it.* A muse is someone who leads you close to what you want, right up to the glass.

"No," I'd replied, and it was true. Only later did I realize what I did want, namely, to be that baby myself. I was jealous of X. I was jealous of his fat satisfaction, his trust, the way he gazed—unblinkingly, full of tolerance—at the blurred ovoids of his parents' faces above him. And even if I did love X, he certainly didn't need me to. And so for the most part, I didn't show it. Thus far in our story I thought no one had noticed this, this not-showing-of-love. After all, with Eli gone—for as you recall, by then he really had broken up with me and I was responsible for that, too—who was there to do the noticing? If a tree falls in the forest, and so on?

The answer: Pavia. Who herself was falling, also.

I strolled my nephew to the park, a trapezoidal piece of real estate where several streets converge in the awkward way characteristic of our historic city. According to the man who steered the motorized aerator around three times a year, the ground in this park is harder than in any other place in the U.S. Only a few other places in the entire world—sites along the road to Mecca, the dirt around Jim Morrison's Parisian grave—have soil so compacted. "And yet," he had told me one day with a raised voice, hand resting on the vibrating bar of the aerating machine, "And yet here we still manage to grow grass. Most places can't grow grass. We grow the grass DESPITE the soil compaction!"

The aerator guy wasn't there that evening, of course, though I thought of him as I wheeled the stroller over the turd-like soil plugs strewn across the lawn in a way that made me think of the word *aftermath*. We headed toward the little pond, right up to the concrete-lined edge. The ducks churned below us as I threw breadcrumbs and X waved his fat hands in vicious delight. Later, we walked to the falafel truck parked on the north side of the park. I ordered a sandwich, and the guy leaned far over the steel counter to inspect my nephew.

"Well, he is needing some bread, too!" the man cried, flipping a piece of pita bread like a Frisbee onto X's lap and smiling hugely beneath his impressive mustache. "His beautiful mother cannot be eating everything, and he eating nothing!"

"I was going to share," I said too loudly. "Anyway, he sometimes chokes," I added.

X and I continued our long, meandering route through the park and then throughout our neighborhood. I rested my falafel sandwich on the stroller canopy, picking off bits as we went, making it last longer. I pointed out the local features to my nephew.

> *On your left is the place where your mom fills her
> prescriptions.*
> *There's our newsstand.*
> *There's where my friend Cassandra once saw Madonna
> buying soap.*
> *Straight ahead is a dog like General.*

Just as the sun was going down, we walked past the cooperative community garden. There, the co-opers were having one of their series of self-congratulatory events—*We're organically and with reverence acknowledging the Summer Solstice!*—and they had the white fairy lights up, and somebody was playing clarinet, and there were hugs and shoulder squeezes all around. And looking on with X—my little fake son, my prop and proof, my temporary responsibility—I felt momentarily appropriate, like someone who might herself one day begin a small composting effort. A baby, after all, is very natural, very local, as real and heavy as a clod of dirt compressed. A baby is too new to have mental health issues. No one breaks up with a baby or just "takes a break"—or so I thought.

I took X out of the stroller and held him to me as we stood outside the chain link fence around the garden. I swayed with the music rising up to the faded moon above. X grabbed for my glasses, then hooked his fingers in my mouth and pulled, chortling so adorably and audibly at my grimace that the co-opers were compelled to see us and wave us in, implying *our neighborhood garden is a place of welcome!* I shook my head *no thanks*, but stayed there for a few more minutes. In fact, I lingered. I was of course avoiding going home to Pavia's, where the heavy dread of loneliness awaited me, the aftermath of a long day that was itself a sort of aftermath, deserved, of all my selfishness.

Thus it was late, well past X's bedtime, when I finally pointed the stroller's grimy wheels toward home. And when I arrived at the apartment—having dragged the stroller backwards up the steps with X still in it, him holding onto the bar in front with two knob-like fists and shuddering at each banging vertical increment—and as I opened the door with the wet key I'd been holding in my mouth, I was surprised that the red light of the answering machine wasn't on. I thought Pavia would have called by then.

Onward I went into baby care: bottle, diaper change, pajamas. I rocked X in the chair that Jack, red-faced with embarrassed pride and the strain of carrying forty pounds of crafted pinewood up from the car, had bought the week before his son was born. X, bless him, fell asleep quickly as I rocked him. Like his mother, he slept with his eyes slightly open, two slivers of blue-white sclera gleaming beneath his black eyelashes. I laid my nephew in his crib, and crept backwards out of the bedroom, a reverse thief.

Downstairs, all the lights were off. The streetlights extruded perfect rectangles of light through the front windows and onto the floor, catching the poles and sails of the stroller parked in the hallway as with a storied shipwreck. General got up unsteadily from his bed by the fireplace, did a lap around the couch, and thudded back down again. I sat down on the couch and grabbed the remote, and when I turned the TV on the note taped to its front glowed supernaturally.

This is what my sister had written:

Thea,

I'm going away for a few days. Take care of Xavier. There's instructions taped to the inside of the cupboard door (coffee cupboard).

There's frozen breastmilk. Use the oldest first—the bags have dates on them. Don't microwave to thaw.

I'm going to get out for a few days.

Don't freak. Don't call Jack. Don't call the Reeds. I'M ONLY TAKING A BREAK. Let's say I'll be gone for four days. So you'll have to get off work. Jack thinks we're visiting Supernal so he won't come this week don't worry. Daycare knows too— Xavier's out for the week.

My baby loves his auntie very much and his mommy gives him kisses to last until she comes home.

Sorry.

Thanks.

Anyway, you know it's fair.

XO Pavia

P.S. Really don't call Jack. I won't call you because I don't want to hear it. Which is why I didn't ask beforehand. Good luck. Love my baby. You can do it.

I read the note again. The third time through I stroked General lying at my side, one long pat for each line of Pavia's note, grateful to have his bulk and meager intelligence at my side.

"She doesn't mention you at all, General," I told the dog. With each dumb breath in, his soft back rose against my hand. I got up and turned the TV off. I went to lock the front door. As I twisted the key and felt the deadbolt slide across, I made myself say it out loud. *She's coming back.*

Later.

27. A CANADIAN CLUB

A mushroom walks into a bar and the bartender says, "We don't serve your kind here," and the mushroom says, "Why not? I'm a fungi."

A horse walks into a bar, and the bartender says, "Why the long face?"

A baby seal walks into a bar, and the bartender asks, "What can I get you?" and the baby seal says, "Anything but a Canadian Club."

A man walks into a bar and says, "Ow!"

A woman—Dorothy—walks into a bar. She's got cash. She wants to buy a round for everyone. Joseph is there, and there she also meets people with names like "Gypsy" and "Peyote." She plays pool; she has her palm read. She tries tequila. She asks the bartender for a double entendre and he gives it to her. She leaves the bar with a man. Or two.

Yo mama's so old, she was the waitress at the Last Supper.
Yo mama's so fat, she fell in love and broke it.
Yo mama's so crazy, she kept you.

Laughter. Do you get it, my daughter?
Nothing else is truer, and nothing else is more important.

28. THE DAY IN SMALL PARTS

As I've maintained, on the night Pavia left I thought I'd just be babysitting for the evening. But then I came home from the walk and found the note. And the scene where I stand in the doorway of the darkened room and gaze at X in his crib for untold minutes—as if in a spell of measureless affection and personal resolve to bravery ultimately broken only by the impulse to pull the blanket up around his little quivering chin—didn't happen next.

Nor did it develop that I called Jack that very moment, who sped over—nostrils flaring as if to better catch the scent of the argument he would later use in the pitched custody battle—to claim X while the girl from Marketing sat in his car and looked up at the front of the house, the front steps of which featured me, holding General by his collar as if to prevent his attack.

Also not occurring: Eli suddenly at the door, looking exhausted and chagrined, saying that he didn't want to be away from me at all any more, then reaching for me like a door marked PULL and me swinging forward easily.

Instead I watched the end of *Dances with Wolves* on TV and, sedated, went to bed in my room. X woke me up in the night, crying. After that I slept every night in Pavia's bed, listening to X's humid respiration next to me in the crib. When I woke up in the mornings, my nephew would often be sitting up and looking at me critically through the bars. We were both thinking about Pavia, I knew.

She is coming back, I reminded myself.

And thus each of these daytimes began and then continued until nighttime. Open and shut. There were seconds, minutes, and hours in each of these days in which to wonder about the purpose or cause or normalcy of X's behavior or appearance (as my responsibility, he was newly foreign to me), but I followed Pavia's written instructions faithfully, and thus I was kept occupied.

This helped. The business of infant care required my arms and back and legs as I lifted and carried and walked and walked and walked. Guilt and dread and loneliness covered me like the radiologist's trusty lead apron, but I kept moving. I worked. I had X; I had to. And by the fourth day, each part of the day—which I began to think of as "our" day, was do-able, I found. Pavia was coming back, and we could live the day in small parts and get through till then.

For example: Unit 1 was initial diapering and feeding and getting dressed. Unit 2 was activity—goofing off on a spread-out blanket with a few chew toys, or hanging out in the exersaucer— and it concluded with another bottle and a nap. Unit 3 began with diapering but was otherwise identical to Unit 2. Unit 4 was the evening, and we always went out for a stroll. It was cool in the evening, and there was always the chance that something had changed in the world that we should know about, for example the fact that everyone was evacuating because of a disaster or threat of some kind, and I had failed to hear the sirens during our day's earlier Units 2 and 3. In this case, I would need to put aside our charting and catch a ride out of the big city somehow. And I had begun to think that I could do that. I had packed a bag—a black plastic sack, with diapers and wipes, clothes and formula—just in case.

Six days passed, twenty-four units. We were doing well. Pavia was coming back. Probably the next day.

I was scrupulously following the typed list of care instructions Pavia had taped to the cupboard door. I consulted the books she'd left in a stack near the sink. Still, alone with her infant I had entered a thick vapor of doubt, a Cloud of Unknowing.

X's face turned red, then back to pale again. Why?

He had a scratch beside his eye. Dangerous?

Normal? His scalp had yellow shingles in one place.

X jerked himself awake and cried. And then later he was crying again and I couldn't make him stop. This was necessary, a normal neural reorganization? He was overstimulated? He was tired? Life to him seemed pointless and so much of it still to go?

Thus in those early days alone with X I theorized, every hour. And I was reminded of what a certain kind of celebrity Buddhist—the kind who writes a book called *Vast Compassion, Small Mall*—called the Superball Mind, wherein a very small and sometimes colorful idea bounces between the inside surfaces of the brain, losing momentum and force only very, very gradually. This is exhausting; still, the mind springs to even-more active metaphors: you want to bounce the idea off someone else, check in with them, walk them through it, run it up the flagpole, try it out on them. You want *to share your concern.*

But I had no one to talk to and quickly I developed speculation fatigue. I thought about asking Cassandra to come over, but I didn't. She seemed a little afraid of babies. And anyway, I didn't want to have to talk about Eli.

I wanted to talk *to* Eli. I wanted to ask him if he thought it was okay to put sunscreen on Xavier when the bottle said *Not For Infants Under 6 Months Of Age.*

Also, I wanted to know if dog food might be toxic to babies.

If an emery board could safely be chewed.

If Xavier was crying for a reason, and if so, what was the reason.

If he thought Pavia was all right, most likely.

If she would forgive me.

If he (Eli) would forgive me.

Where my sister was; why I pictured her in a hotel room sitting on the bed; why this image moved inside me like a small ball thrown hard.

If Pavia wasn't all right, what next?

I wanted to ask Eli all of these things, and everything.

The first night that Pavia left me alone with her son, when I'd woken up in the middle of the night, the sound and the understanding came slowly, then tore through me.

Crying. X was crying and had been crying. I hadn't heard.

I went to him of course, as quickly as I could. I pulled him from his crib, held him—took him downstairs and fed him a bottle of Pavia's milk. But when he had finished he started to cry again and though I offered him another bottle I couldn't make him stop. I walked him in circles in the front room. The streetlights forced shadows over us—the hand-like shapes of the leaves outside—in gray and green, anemic.

I had been told that babies always cry for a reason—they're hungry, they're wet, their foot is jammed in the space between the couch and the floor—and that I could discover it. On the other hand, I had also read that babies cry for no reason at all; they sometimes can't be fixed.

X cried and cried, and I didn't know if he had a reason. I

wondered if Pavia would have known.

Once as a kid, Pavia asked Walter—our father—what he wanted for his birthday. He answered her, "A gun. One that would fit inside my mouth."

Pavia, eleven years old at the time, had simply shaken her head. *No.*

She could tell the difference: crying for a reason, or for nothing.

She'd shaken her head *no* and walked away.

Over the years, whenever anyone would ask me or Pavia if we had gotten along as children, we would either say yes or tell this story.

We were at home and Dorothy was in the back bedroom and Pavia and I were arguing in the living room. We were shouting at each other, and then somehow we were wrestling. Pavia always says that we were fighting for possession of something—the *TV Guide?*—but I can't remember what I wanted. Everything? I only remember that I hated her.

So we were on the carpet, gripped in each other's arms as in an allegory. We scraped and clawed; we rolled into a lamp, the couch. She was hurting me. And then with a shove she broke free of me. And she looked plainly at me. And she lay back down.

I quickly scrambled on top of her and grabbed at her head. Her hair came away in my fist, the strands waving with the slight weight of the blood at the root. Pavia lay under me with her eyes squeezed shut. My knees were on either side of her ribs, and together our breathing pushed out and in like two things trapped in a small cage, and I had her hair in my hand.

Pavia tells it, "She ripped my hair out and I gave up!"

Similarly I say, "I made her give!" But I know that's not the truth. I didn't force her; she chose. I scared her, and she wanted to know if I would stop.

We were still looking at my full hand, amazed, when Dorothy called again from the back of the house, "Girls, work it out!" And Pavia looked up from my fist and smiled, open-mouthed, amazed at me.

As the units with X passed, I did not call Jack. And as hour-by-hour X was not perishing or even visibly suffering under my exclusive care, I decided this not-calling was appropriate. Pavia's note had said not to; it had said she might be gone for as long as a week. I could wait that long. I worked through the units with my nephew, and as I did so I allowed myself to become interested.

To wit: Xavier rolling under the coffee table, wetting its legs with his seeking gums. Xavier's martyred, sanguinal expression as he completed a bowel movement. The strength of his grip on General's tail, and on my finger.

In fact I found I liked to put my index fingers in his fists, and rev, rev, rev them like tiny handlebars. *Get your motor runnin'*. He seemed to like that song. *Head out on the highway!*

And how he smiled when I spoke in the funny voice I had just devised—Xavier, my little invention! I found that I could make him laugh.

My sister had disappeared and my boyfriend had rejected me, and now there was yet a new reason to mourn these developments—a reason I kept shoving away with a decisive mental gesture akin to the Stop-in-the-Name-of-Love arrest: no one but me would remember Xavier, or me with him, from these six days in the summer of 1994. When, despite everything, I made him laugh! When he learned to reach for me! When he was perfect—a baby, unhurt, temporary.

I reminded myself that someday Xavier would be a teenager. His feet would smell and he would likely have pimples on his back; a few coarse, pale whiskers might poke from his shiny chin. By then he would know that I am neither interesting, nor funny, nor physically appealing. Nor would I find him so at that stage, perhaps.

Still. I began to know that I would always remember Xavier as he was these six days, these two-hundred and four hours, those dozens of units of time alone together. I would remember how it was when the clenched strands of my affection finally relaxed and drifted out over my small nephew's body like glass noodles, like jellyfish tentacles, like spider silk, like unfolding proteins. When I took care of my genetic material, I fell in love.

So now, after all, comes the scene where I stand in the doorway of the darkened bedroom and gaze at Xavier. But in the scene I wasn't thinking of him after all. I was thinking of his mother, and of his mother's mother—your grandmother, Dorothy.

I looked in at the crib. I reached out on both sides to grip the doorjamb. I was feeling the wave that had caught Pavia and Dorothy—impulses toward escape, desperate convictions, a terrible and energizing dismay after joy—and for a moment, it pulled me backward, too. But I held on. The wave passed, and ordinary sadness washed back into the room around me.

Xavier sighed and turned over, his fat cheek bulged against the mattress. I wanted to cover him again with his blanket but I couldn't get to the crib. I couldn't let go of the doorjamb. I was holding on, thinking hard about Pavia, thinking hard to tell her hold on, too. *Come back.*

29. I LOOK FORWARD TO YOU

What I discovered in this time with Xavier was the vast, eclipsing selfishness of babies, the eventual superfluity of what I'd always thought of as my self. If I was exhausted and afraid, when I was busy or unsure—Xavier didn't care. He wanted what he wanted. Bottle, toy, change, comfort, me.

Now.

Now.

Irradiated by indifference, I felt that I was cured at last. Responsive to treatment. Relieved.

Now. How I look forward to you and your indifference to me! I'm tired of always thinking about myself. I want to be a mother.

30. A CLEANSING BREATH

On the seventh day I had just put Xavier down for a nap when the phone rang.

"It's okay," Jack said as soon as I picked up. "I've got her. Pavia."

I couldn't say anything. The faint music from Xavier's mobile—theme from *Doctor Zhivago*—wound down on the other side of the closed door like a bad actor in a death scene. I put one hand up against the wall and listened.

Jack went on: Pavia had been staying at a hotel at an Indian casino outside of the city. She had used the pool a lot, ate at the buffet. She had watched a lot of TV. The static on the upper channels, the empty ones—channels eighty, eighty-one, eighty-two—brought back to her the rasping nothingness of the baby monitor, and milk would wet her shirt painfully. Finally she had called Jack.

"Help," he said she'd said.

"I'm going to bring her home," he said, ridiculously. By then I knew that this is the sort of thing one might say when one is responsible for someone else—the obvious, the technically unnecessary—a remark akin to *I'm right here, Xavier,* which I myself had just completed saying, so I forgave Jack.

"I'm going to bring her home," he repeated. "But can you stay with Xavier for another couple of days? We need—we need some time. All right?"

I managed to agree. "Xavier's fine," I added. "Tell Pavia. He's just—" and then tears began to run beneath my glasses frames, down my cheeks into the corners of my mouth turned up in hideous Joker-like delight, "he's perfect."

Jack gave me the name of the hotel and said goodbye without offering to let me talk to Pavia. I hung up.

In front of my eyes: my hand on the wall blurred like someone trembling.

Pavia was safe, and gratitude made me giddy, greedy. Suddenly more than ever, I wanted everything.

"Xavier!" When he awoke I greeted him with my teeth bared. He was my blood. When I kissed his cheeks the feel of them on my lips made me want to eat him, smash him, smother him, smear him all over me in an act of ecstatic vandalism.

Or feed him at my breast, or become him.

Or fall into him through the torn flecks in his yellow-brown eyes.

Or read and memorize him, backwards and forwards, verbatim.

And thus inevitably I was reminded that I couldn't love him like I wanted to. It wasn't because he wasn't my own son or because my childhood had rendered me incapable of deep attachments and healthy expressions thereof. It wasn't because there was something wrong with me or that I was a loser in love.

Rather, I saw that it was impossible. We would always fall short. We would get closer but would never arrive; we were lines striving for zero, asymptotic.

The rain in Spain falls mainly on the plain. In Hartford, Hereford, and Hampshire, hurricanes hardly ever happen.

I thought of Pavia's stoppered cry as Xavier was pulled out of her body, and her look of defeat as they placed him in her arms. I thought of her in the townhouse in the days before she left, wordlessly packing away more of Jack's belongings. I remembered all the silences spliced into every conversation with Dorothy and Walter, all the sad gaps added in. Now, by George, I got it. We put them there—all the empty parts—so that love could be overdubbed later, once we got it right.

I'm getting it, I thought with a slow and humbling surprise. *I can.*

I had told my supervisor, Charmaine, that I was having a family emergency and needed time off, and her voice on the phone —hushed, eager, Deeply Sorry—told me to take as much time as I needed. Still, when Monday morning came and Pavia and Jack were still not back, I decided to clean up Xavier and myself and go into work.

I'd seen this sort of thing done before: women on maternity leave turning up with their babies for lunch with the old gang, looking newly exfoliated and impressionable. I wanted to keep feeling new, too, rather than afraid. So in to work I came with Xavier, my little distraction.

And maybe I also knew that Eli might be there.

I pushed Xavier in his stroller along the hallways between the cubicles and window offices. The wheels were silent on the padded commercial carpet. And as I rolled into our department on the 21st floor, Xavier gurgled in a wet and unmistakably infantile way, prompting my coworkers to begin to poke up like otoscopes over the top of the cubicle walls, beaming at us with focused delight.

They gathered around us, my fellow medical writers. Flint, the pear-shaped grammarian, hitched up his trousers and declared Xavier "exceptional." Tina, who decorated our break room for every holiday including President's Day, flapped her hands in a curious, special-needs way, recalling her own children at that age (more hair, less chubby, real handfuls). Charmaine swung her bolt of long red hair to the opposite shoulder as she bent down and lifted Xavier up out of the stroller. She set him up on the ledge of her bony hip and looked around at the rest of us expectantly.

"He likes me," she told us.

Flint and Tina nodded. It seemed to be true. Xavier was smiling at her, open-mouthed. So was I, I realized, my mouth flooding with saliva in a way analogous to the way my heart was suddenly awash with gratitude for my nephew's undeniable appeal, which he'd inherited from his mother, who would be coming home soon, all better.

"He does like you!" I said, swallowing hard, and at the sound of my voice my perfect nephew twisted toward me and held out his arms to me.

"Awww," said Tina and Flint. Charmaine handed him over.

We chatted for a few more minutes. I patched up the explanatory screen for Pavia's absence—"family issues; Jack's side of the family"—and related, in an excess of detail, how Xavier and I spent our days at home together. Flint, Tina, and Charmaine cooed and prodded at Xavier, my irresistible exhibit. Xavier—my lanyard badge, my key indicator, my action item, my initial public offering! When I heard Charmaine's phone ring in her office, I realized with a start that I should leave the office now, while I was still feeling interesting and reassured.

"Naptime," I sighed, and I stowed Xavier back in the seat

of the stroller.

"Bye-bye," I said, and everyone repeated after me—Flint loudest of all, his heels rising up from the insoles of his loafers—waving their fingers at us until I turned and started back down the hall toward the elevators.

With straight-armed discipline, I pushed the stroller along, watching the rubber wheels pick up lint and some resistance on the carpeting. I was calculating the number of baggies of breastmilk we had left in the freezer at home when I rounded the last cubicle corner by the elevators and the stroller stopped with a sudden muted *klonk*. The stroller wheels had hit the wheels of Eli's plant-watering cart. And Eli was looking at Xavier—with surprise, of course, but not with distaste—and then up at me.

Klonk.

"Hey," Eli said. "I was going to call you." He wiped his chin with the back of his hand, then bent down briefly, reaching for something on his cart. He lifted his camera up to his face and twisted the lens to focus it on us. He clicked the shutter.

Eli lowered the camera, *klonk*, and reached forward to take my hand in his. He pressed. Xavier let out a single happy, pointless scream. "Anyway," Eli said, smiling a little, "I've got you now."

As it happened, I decided to feed Xavier in the break room while Eli finished up with the plants, and then the three of us left the office building together. I pushed the stroller and Eli carried Xavier, who fell asleep on his shoulder. We stopped to put a blanket over Xavier. Eli and I walked all the way back to the townhouse without talking, a kabuki journey—all my movements strangely intentional, my face bloodless under the theatrical sun as I waited for what would happen between us.

Back at the townhouse, we put Xavier down to sleep in his crib. We lay down on Pavia's big bed beside him; we lowered our shoes to the floor. Eli and I turned toward each other on our sides and wove our sweaty fingers together. I pulled my glasses off and set them unfolded on an open book on the nightstand, as if to let them read on without me…. I looked at the skin on Eli's clavicle, his pulse in his neck. I didn't meet his eyes but I let him look at me.

Time passed, as it does. We listened to Xavier's little snufflings and movements—just as we will, very soon now, listen to yours—and then we fell asleep with a sudden muted *klonk*.

The phone was ringing. I sat up and looked over at Xavier, who was sitting up in his crib staring at me. He looked over at the phone; I picked it up.

"Pavia?" Walter coughed percussively in my ear.

"No, it's me."

"Put her on," my father said.

"It's only—" I looked at the clock on Pavia's nightstand "—it's only four in the afternoon."

"She's at work? How come you're not?"

"Well, she would be, but she's out of town. Business trip." I had rehearsed this.

Walter coughed some more, ending in a disgusted-sounding *Jesus Christ*.

"I'll give her a message," I told him. Now Eli was awake, too, and he reached through the bars of the crib to tweeze Xavier's toes with his thumb and forefinger. "What's the message?"

My father coughed. Presumably the matted cilia in his lungs shrugged, convulsed.

"Judith died!" Walter finally shouted. "Okay?! Goodbye."

He hung up. I moved Eli's hand off of my thigh and dialed my father back.

He answered on the first ring. His voice was thick and low.

"Yeah?"

"Dad. How? I'm sorry."

"Got sick," he said. "Pneumonia."

"When?"

"Last night," he said. "Hospital. I was there."

I pictured my father's long back, bent over in a chair next to her bed in a greenish room. He would have wanted to smoke. He would have wanted not to be there, once again, watching the weaker sex succumb. "How come?" I asked.

My father tried to take a deep breath, coughed, and then was quiet. "I asked for your sister just now," he said finally. "She knew Judith better. She could have told you. That would have been fine."

I pictured my father at the 3Bee's, no one across from him in the booth. He was an old man watching the waitress move from table to table with the coffee pot.

"Dad," I said, my throat squeezing in.

Then we were each just holding our respective phone receivers and making small human sounds; no words. The heavy plastic against my cheek felt greasy and warm; it was connected across two thousand miles to my father. Eli watched me, his fingers wiggling through the crib bars toward Xavier, waiting.

"Well," I said finally. "I guess I can tell Pavia then."

"Do that, Thea," he said, and hung up.

I leaned down over the edge of the bed and opened Eli's camera bag. I lifted the camera out of its little foam coffin and took off the lens cap. I put the camera to my wet face and focused the lens. I took a picture of Eli and Xavier touching fingers through the bars of the crib; then I took another one.

Three days passed in which Eli and I practiced co-parenting and the denial of self-reflection that this required. In other words,

Eli went to work and I stayed home and together we cared for the baby and didn't talk about our relationship; we were busy. Jack called every day, his voice gradually sounding more steady. He gave what he called a status report: Pavia was doing better; her outlook was improving; they would soon be home. I never spoke to my sister and I was grateful that Jack did not suggest it.

They came home on Thursday evening. The three of us—Eli, me, Xavier—were in the kitchen when they arrived. Xavier was in his high chair, moistening the perimeter of a slice of toast, and Eli and I were on either side of him at the table eating bowls of cereal. We heard the front door open, shoe heels on the hallway floor, and then Pavia came into the kitchen wearing a new red dress. Jack trailed behind like a parade float, carrying in his big arms Pavia's duffle bag and two sacks of groceries.

Without saying a word Pavia came forward, leaned down and buried her face in Xavier's negligible neck, blindly unbuckling his high-chair seat belt with one hand. Then she lifted him up and out and fit him onto her waist in front. His short, fat legs barely reached to her sides, his arms floated up. She looked at him searchingly. Xavier smiled politely back at her, then looked around for his toast, which he had dropped on the floor.

Eli reached down for the toast. Jack put the bags down on the floor and took the toast from him. I stood up. I said a few things loudly and unmemorably; I waved my hands like a baby. Jack gave me a hug.

"You two are back on?" Jack asked Eli, shaking his hand. "Back in the fold?"

Eli opened his mouth to say something, then shrugged.

Jack clapped him on the shoulder, moved on. "You two? Did you take good care of my son?"

Eli pointed at me. "All her."

"All me, all the time," I said. I sighed shakily and tried a fresh smile.

Now there was a silence. It was a unit of time overfull with the still-rising relief and the fear it nevertheless contained, the *what if*.

"We ended up at Lake Winnipesauke." Pavia's voice was the same as ever—lowish, assured-sounding. She pulled Xavier into her chest and faced me and Eli. "Jack's folks' timeshare." She shook her hair off her forehead, and there it was at last: a small smile from her, one compatible with fear. "Did Jack tell you...? We're together?"

"Yeah." Eli and I answered together like a pair of backup singers, the *What Ifs*.

Now Jack moved in on his wife and son to form a more symmetrical nativity scene, the miraculous child at the center, the overhead light on the ceiling burning like a steady star.

"And lo," I said. "Tidings of great joy." Eli stepped closer and put his arm around me.

"What do you mean?" Pavia's eyes widened slightly. "You're not...pregnant? Are you?" She looked at Eli.

I quickly shook my head. "Just glad you're back. Xavier missed you." At his mother's waist, Xavier grasped her dark hair and frowned with concentration. I could almost feel his body on my own hip again, his imperial heaviness. Xavier, my former prerogative, my phantom limb....

"You okay?" Eli asked into my ear. He pressed my shoulders against his side.

"Thea?" Pavia's smile subsided as she looked at me.

A person in ill repair in many ways, I couldn't help the leaking tears and the way my face—that bad contraption—was breaking down in bits and parts.

"Eeeh," Xavier commented, glancing over at me.

I took what Dorothy calls a Cleansing Breath and wiped my

cheeks up under my glasses with my fingers.

"He was wonderful," I said after a minute, pointing accusingly at my nephew. "He was...fantastic. I loved taking care of him."

Everyone beamed at me with approval and relief. But my finger and forearm were slowly swiveling like a construction crane toward my sister.

"And you can't do that again." I pointed at her. "You can't." I towered, I swayed, I threatened to topple as I waited.

My beautiful sister stared back at me and nodded. "I kind of lost it," she said. Still, her voice was just the same.

Now I pointed at Jack, and now back again at Pavia.

"Well, you can't," I said. "Jack? Pavia?"

"Thea," Pavia said.

We all waited; it was Pavia's turn to take a Cleansing Breath, which seemed to work well and rapidly.

"I didn't know what to do." Pavia squeezed Xavier on her hip, and nodded toward Jack. "I needed to get Jack back."

"Ha!" I barked, "That rhymes." My stupid finger now pointed to the ceiling. "Make a new plan, Stan!"

My sister held her son and inhaled; she pulled him close and kissed the back of his head. Jack twisted the wristband of his watch, no doubt catching his arm hairs painfully.

"We can't afford to have you lose it," I said. My voice had the authority of an angry infant. "All of you! Stay sane."

General, who had had his nose in Pavia's crotch, sat down immediately and looked up at me. While she was gone I had taught him how to stay.

"Okay," Eli said finally. He smiled at me gently. "But you know, you're sounding kind of crazy yourself."

I stuck my fingers behind my glasses again, and I pressed until the scribbled stars inside my head came out against my eyelids. Eventually, I laughed. When I put my hands down and my vision had clarified, Pavia was looking at me with one hand outstretched and her little finger extended. I reached out to hook my little finger around hers.

"Promise," I said, sniffling. "You won't flip out again."

Pavia squeezed my finger tighter. "You, too." She looked at me with a new gentleness, a loveliness, a maternal resignation, a sadness that would last forever. Both of us have always believed that I'm crazier than she is—maybe even worse than Dorothy—because I am always angry, always wanting. But maybe we were wrong. "I'll try," she said.

I nodded, we shook pinkies on it, and I hugged my sister, compressing her small son between us with dispersed firm pressure. Xavier stayed still, intersticed by genetically similar flesh, his own heart beating and tiny lungs filling and emptying. So far, still, he was in perfect working order.

"Break it up," Jack said at last. "This meeting is adjourned." He stepped forward and held his arms out. I walked into them before I realized he wasn't trying to hug me.

"No, no, no," he laughed, putting me aside. "Hand him to his daddy!" He lifted Xavier off Pavia's body and held him high overhead. Xavier squealed and a silver exclamation point fell from his open mouth onto Jack's forehead.

Eli and I decided to go back to his apartment that night. Walking toward the subway with nothing but my backpack—that is, without Xavier and his dry goods and transport devices—I felt oddly light and vulnerable, like a blown-out egg.

With both arms I hugged Eli around his waist. I lurched sideways beside him, then gave that up. He put his arm around me. He kissed my cheek for half a block, his nose moving up and down against my cheekbone as we went. It was a beautiful night, warm and quiet except for the noise of a domestic dispute—*You fucking always do this to me!*—sifting down from the top floor of a building across the street.

"Hey," I said.

"Hey," Eli answered back.

I dropped back behind him and began to kick the soles of his shoes forward as we went.

"Why—did—you—want—me—back?" Eli's legs jerked forward like a marionette's as I kicked his shoes.

"Knock it off," he said. I surged forward and lifted his arm back across my shoulders. We didn't say anything else for a while. We walked on for another block, shadows from the buildings rolling over us.

"I wanted you back," I said, and as I heard the words I felt a sickening thrill, like seeing blood blooming from a new cut.

"I missed you," I continued, bloodthirsty and dismayed. "I love you."

We walked some more and I couldn't bear to look at him. Systolic pressure dropping, I covered his hand on my shoulder with my own hand.

"Are you still mad at me?"

"Yeah," he said. He pointed to a bench at a bus stop and we sat down. With my backpack still on, I could only fit half my butt on the seat until Eli grabbed the straps and pulled my pack off. He put it on the ground between his sneakers and pulled me close to him. He rested his chin on top of my head.

"I'm still pissed that you lied about the birth control." His voice buzzed through the bones of my skull.

"But?" I prompted, keeping my head still.

"But I missed you."

I gazed at a flattened drink cup in the curb in front of us, marveling at its beauty. Its waxy side caught the light from the streetlamp and held it up generously, variably, like luminous cells under a microscope, turning and dividing.

"And?" I asked.

"Look. I've been to art school, community college, and a welder's training course. I've been in two rock bands; I've held about twenty shitty jobs. I'm shooting photos for some reason, but I'll never make any money at it. And…I don't know."

"You're looking for a steady." I was glad that our embrace didn't allow me to see his face. We seemed to be communicating better than usual, our skulls stacked up as if in a catacomb somewhere, chatting away our eternity.

"No," Eli said. "Well, sort of. It's not about having security. I mean, I don't think all of this should be easy, necessarily."

"It won't be," I said quickly and with just a small note of panic.

"I mostly go from thing to thing. I've never wanted something the way you seem to want this."

I waited. A bus approached the stop; I felt Eli wave it past.

"This?" I said finally, crazily, responsibly.

"A baby," he said, his chin hard across my sagittal suture.

I shook my head and sat up to face him. It hurt, actually hurt—the hope that surged through me like a hormone. I took a cleansing breath again, why not? Maybe I could make room for it.

"You want to hitch your wagon to my senseless desperation?"

He smiled slowly at me, and I saw it: probably, he loved me.

"I guess," Eli said.

It hurt some more, that hope. I said, "I don't even know why I want a baby." I thought about it; I swallowed. I considered cataloguing the vast inventory of my unmet emotional needs, and

213

decided not to. Nothing else came to mind to say. It was Eli's turn.

"But you want it so much. I saw it with Xavier."

I nodded.

"I do, too," he said. "I mean mostly, I want the wanter."

I closed my eyes and turned my face up toward his, my tongue prepping gratefully inside my mouth and my hands grabbing for his belt loops.

And this kiss was just the way I had always dreamed it would be, backlit by sadness, edged with it, my funny valentine, my luck.

31. ON NOT GIVING UP

Is it true that if you dare to dream it, you can become it? In the bedroom I shared with my sister as a child, I had a poster of a ballerina that bore this claim; it was tacked to the drywall, just above the grease rainbow left by my head on the pillow. Pavia's side of the room had the poster of the kitten hanging from a tree branch: *Hang In There.*

Do good things come to those who wait and/or does slow and steady win the race? Is success 99% perspiration? What is the true power of positive thinking? If, for example, you face a fatal diagnosis bravely, visualizing good-cell warriors strafing the malignancy, never giving up, remaining surpassingly grateful for and attentive to friends, family, the Simple Pleasures of Every New Day—under these circumstances, whom do you blame when it becomes clear that you are going to die anyway and maybe very painfully?

As you know, I took care of your cousin Xavier for a week by myself when he was a baby. Pavia was gone. And as I was dressing him one morning, pulling his big head through the neck-hole of his onesie, he suddenly jerked his arms such that his right hand—with its soft and half-frayed fingernails—slashed my left eye. I hadn't put my glasses on yet.

I yelled. My eye was on fire. I thought I would be blind, my eye just an X scratched over the O.

Xavier, his head newly emerged from his clothing, began to scream too. Mouth like a megaphone, round eyes amplifying fear. He fought to get away from me as I held him on the bed.

Now remember: *he* hurt *me*. I was the one who deserved to cry. I was crying first! Nevertheless, I had to comfort Xavier and I did, saline pouring down my face. He hit and kicked me further, full of contempt for me as I held him, shushed him, let him pull on my earrings while I leered at him like a pirate with my one good eye. Gradually he calmed down. Xavier, my little changeling, my animal familiar, my minor defeat.

Still, I wasn't done crying. I meant to get back to it later, once Xavier was down for his nap. My eye hurt like a mother. Also by then I knew that Pavia really had left me, and that I couldn't stop her or help her.

How I looked forward to it, to that moment alone when I could cry for myself! But I never got around to it. I suppose I gave up on it.

So back to our question: what about your hopes and dreams? Can you become whatever you want to become?

I don't know.

My advice: Don't be the person who won't try. But don't be the person who won't give up, either.

32. UNPROTECTED

Sensibly, Jack moved back in to the townhouse. I moved in with Eli and Cassandra. General and Xavier stayed put of course, and I missed them. I missed their bodies—their warmth, their poorly controlled limbs and overlong nails, their slobbering joy at seeing me come through the door at the end of the day. I missed the way Xavier, his head heavy against my sternum as I carried him to his crib at night, had pressed into me the weird joy of overwhelming responsibility. Still, I had another responsibility, just as weird: to keep thinking that Pavia would get better and stay that way, and more generally, a kind of hope for myself.

Now, in the new living arrangement, Eli would roll off me breathing hard. He would look at me in the dim light of his bedroom. He would reach beneath the mattress and pluck a condom out with two fingers. He would hold it up.

I would smile, shrug. I no longer thought I should be the one to choose. My bare shoulders rose and fell.

Eli held the package up—the little square of purple paper with its suggestive circle in the middle—then let it drop to the floor unopened. He smiled and pushed my knees apart with two hands the way a gunslinger comes through the doors of a saloon. The ragtime music stopped, then started up again, louder than before.

Thus we continued, unprotected in our love, and like every Anonymous who ever wrote to *Penthouse Letters*, incredulously.

Dorothy rolled over in bed and looked at the red letters on the clock radio. 11:37 a.m. Still in her clothes from the day before, one half of her hairdo pushed up, she sighed and twisted up to a sitting position. She sat there for a moment above her folded legs like that crippled girl Christina, the one in Wyeth's famous painting, the one left out on the prairie to get some air, presumably.

Dorothy looked through the open door of the bedroom down the hall. She was listening for my knock at the front door, which she kept locked.

Dorothy slowly stretched her legs straight and got herself out of bed. She padded down the hall. Drawings that Pavia and I had done were taped askew along both sides, above the bluish smears left by our hands.

Dorothy stood for a moment at the end of the hallway and looked in the kitchen. Our bowls from breakfast were still on the table, the milk yellow with dissolved cereal, thick. The counters were stacked with dishes. The curtain was drawn over the sliding glass door that led to the backyard.

Dorothy turned away, toward the living room and the front entrance. The curtains were drawn there, too, over the picture windows at the front of the house, but there was a gap in the middle. Dorothy went forward and stood in the gap, looking out into the street.

She was looking in the direction of the school, where I would be walking from. Pavia and I were given lunch money every morning, but I couldn't face eating lunch at school. I had no one to sit with. So for most of that year, fourth grade, I'd been walking home instead.

Dorothy stood in the gap of the curtains, feeling half sick. She squinted in the hard winter sunlight coming through the window. She was watching for me. She was waiting to see me in my blue parka coming down the street; I'd have my hood pulled up and my face pointing down.

Dorothy thought about how she would tell me. The problem was that there really was no *good* reason, there was just *a* reason— something like shame, like love. Dorothy couldn't explain. She decided that she would just say to me, *You can't come home for lunch anymore*, and leave it at that.

And during my hurried lunch—the noon break was just 45 minutes long, and it took more than half of this time to walk home and back—that's what she did say to me. She was sitting next to me at the kitchen table with my parka covering her lap like a blanket. "You can't come home for lunch anymore, Thea."

"Why not?" I asked. I was eating more cereal, therefore I held a spoon. Among flatware, spoons are the most comforting, don't you think?

"Because."

I took in my mother's face, her pretty mouth pushed down by heavy cheeks. Her pale skin, green-veined below the eyes. Her eyes facing out from her head like a couple of sad captives.

Because she needed to send me away; because I needed to leave; because she needed to sleep without interruption and she loved me.

I shut my eyes. I opened my mouth and began spooning in Cheerios as fast as I could. "Okay," I said from the side of my mouth, filling up fast.

Xavier was six, seven, eight months old, sitting up by

himself and pointing like a little foreigner on a tour bus, poorly informed but full of winning appreciation. Finally, Pavia convinced Walter to come to the big city to meet his grandson. Dorothy, we all decided, was once again too sick to come.

Jack and I went in his car to pick up Walter. And once we were on the highway, I found myself telling Jack about the time Pavia and I had gone to the airport to see his parents.

"You wouldn't have recognized her," I told him. "She had a white wig. She was sitting in a wheelchair."

Jack didn't seem surprised by this story or even particularly interested. He rubbed one blond eyebrow with his index finger and maintained the car's speed in the middle lane.

"Eli said that that stunt sounds more like something I would do, not Pavia." In fact, Eli hadn't said that. As you know, I lie. "But it was her idea, totally. I was just along for the ride."

Jack, a grownup, kept steering his practical sedan, giving me nothing.

I looked out the window. Billboards, off ramps, blue sky scratched up by contrails. Other cars with other people inside staring elsewhere, inscrutable, their pinkies sometimes tidying the entrance to their nostrils....

I couldn't look at Jack. "Do you know what's wrong with Pavia?" I asked. It wasn't rhetorical. My sister, I had noticed recently, was counting again. Checking, repeating, tapping the backs of the chairs, the tops of the fences, the tiles on the walls of the subway stations.

"The repeating things, you mean," Jack said. "Yeah. Well. I know what she says." He glanced in the rearview mirror, hit the gas, changed lanes, slowed back down again. "She feels like if she doesn't do these things, someone is going to get hurt."

"Xavier?"

"Xavier, me, you, somebody. She knows it's crazy, but she

worries."

"She worries." I repeated it like a child. I thought about it like a child. "She didn't use to worry. She never *seemed* to worry. When we were growing up she didn't worry."

"No?" My brother-in-law gave me a skeptical glance. "Well. I guess there's a time and place for everything."

The molded black plastic of the dashboard, the spongy rubber of the seal around the window, the smell of car interior. "What are you going to do, then?"

Jack shook his head. "Try to watch out for her. Love her. I'll need to be better at these things. What about you?"

The green sign with the airplane shape came at us overhead; I pointed at it. My sister's husband steered us toward the exit.

"The problem is, I sort of agree with her." I put one foot up on the glove compartment, easing lumbar strain. "If she doesn't do things, something bad *will* happen. She really is the one who has to keep it together."

Surprisingly, Jack laughed. "Really? Why is that her job? Aren't you old enough?" He twisted his wrist to check his watch.

"No!" I whined. "It's Pavia!" It was suddenly wonderful, being indulged. "She's the one—she's it," I insisted, "I call *her*." But even as I spoke I knew that probably after all, I was going to be able to give up on this. I'd indulged it long enough.

Then Jack was rolling down the window to take the ticket from short-term parking. "You *call* her? Well, don't. Don't call us, Thea," he laughed back at me over his shoulder. "We'll call you."

Walter stayed for a week, sleeping in Pavia and Jack's second bedroom. During the workweek, with Xavier at daycare, he spent the day at one of the libraries of the world-famous university. "It's quiet, with the uncomfortable chairs I'm used to," he explained. He was taken to the wharf, to a historic cemetery, to a baseball game; one day Eli rode the circular bus route with him to show him the neighborhoods that make up our big city. And Eli and I came for dinner most of the nights that week.

On the last night of his visit, Walter was sitting back from the dinner table, his grandson balanced on his long thighs. He steadied Xavier in a way that called to mind industrial robotics, elbows pivoting for small adjustments and rebalancing maneuvers.

Dinner was over. We were asking him about Dorothy, finally.

"You know?" he shrugged. "She's down or she's up. She sleeps all the time, or never. She calls me to change the batteries in the remote control. I take her grocery shopping. And every few weeks, I drive her to the shrink."

Xavier, crazy-eyed, worked his fingers into my father's arm hairs the way King Midas handled coins.

"Yeah." Walter smiled. "It's for her regular *follow-up*. Assessment of compliance."

"Clinical outcomes," I said. "Functional measures." Pavia dropped her head forward and laughed. We had inherited my father's looks—Pavia more than me, but still—and his sense of humor. We had inherited his contempt and affection for our mother, marbled together like fatty meat. Our father had not been careful with his genetic material.

"Basically, I sit in the car in front of the doctor's office and I honk until she comes back out," Walter said, coughing. We all laughed. Jack refilled our wine glasses. Pavia reached for Xavier and put him to her breast, then looked across the table at her father. "Tell about Judith," she said.

Walter's eyes slid from Pavia to me. He patted the pocket on his t-shirt—reassuring himself that he still had cigarettes in the pack—but he didn't get up. "She was a good friend. I'm going to miss her."

I wiped my mouth. "You used to have coffee with her at the 3Bee's every morning."

"I still go." Walter took a rattling breath in, narrowed his eyes. "I have to," he said. "If I don't have at least three cups of their strong coffee, I can't take a shit."

Eli put his hand on mine; I rubbed my eyes with my free hand. Underneath the overhead lamp, we sat in a circle like a Mongolian family in a yurt, while all of nature howled outside. We listened.

"Thea," Pavia said. "Remember that night of Eli's opening? The gallery exhibit?" She stroked Xavier's back as he nursed.

"You were in the bathroom or something. And I was just standing there with him"—she dipped her chin toward Xavier—"and a guy, maybe mid-forties, kind of grizzled, comes up and stares at Xavier for minute. Then he looks at me and goes, 'Time and child molesters.'"

Pavia smoothed a tuft of Xavier's patchy hair and continued. "I didn't know what he was talking about. 'Time and child molesters,' he says again. And then he *really* looks at me. 'They're a mother's worst nightmare.'"

Jack shook his head. "Jesus."

"Yeah, I know. But no." Now Pavia's hand strummed and strummed across her son's back, the trapezius, the latissimus dorsi, the deltoids, *strum strum*, the old familiar ballad. "I know what he means. Look," she said, looking down at Xavier at her breast. "In a minute, he'll be gone." She smiled unhappily. Or rather—she smiled sorrowfully, full of understanding.

"That's what your mother says now." Walter stood up slowly, reaching for his lighter on the table, pulling his cigarettes from his shirt pocket. "Dorothy says, 'it seems like just yesterday when those little girls were born.'"

When she was a little girl, your grandmother Dorothy took ballet lessons. She used to love to dance.

Dorothy's teacher—middle-aged Madame DeCosse—cut a figure: high heels, rhinestone eyeglasses, black pantsuits cross-hatched with cat fur. In class Madame would scream at the class, consistently get a little hysterical. Actual moisture would glitter in her black and magnified eyes.

"THIS HOUR," she would cry, hammering a tiny white fist into the palm of her other hand, "WILL NEVER COME AGAIN. USE IT!"

Madame was always minutely ahead of the beat, even in adagio; the IMBECILE accompanist lagged. Years later, Dorothy could still see Madame coming at her in the mirror. She could remember her hissing in her ear, FOCUS DOROTHY, WORK! And sometimes, as in a horror movie, she thought she could feel it: Madame's hand pushing her forward, as if to force her forehead onto her leg at the barre.

Your poor grandmother! She knew every minute the time she was losing. She counted it. And it was like a piece of music she had to keep on practicing, the same trying phrases, the same basic steps—and all together the measures never made a dance.

Once again I lay on top of Eli's chest, feeling his heart beating through my breasts. The cooling semen sought egress from between my legs; I slid off Eli and onto my back, knees up, to keep it in.

"You know Pavia's guy?" I said. "The time-and-child-molester guy she told us about? That was Steig, I bet."

"I bet you're right." Eli turned onto his side next to me. He yawned. "He hasn't contacted her at all," he said, meaning Cassandra. Steig had gone back to Israel as soon as the spring semester was over.

"His wife may have had it by now."

"Well, it would be really hard to take," Eli agreed. "I don't blame her. She's supposed to look the other way, pretend she doesn't know about his American girlfriend?"

"I meant her baby," I said, laughing. "By now, his wife may have had *the baby*." I patted Eli with one hand while still gripping my folded-up legs with the other. "Did Pavia tell you what my dad said about you, on his last night here?" I asked.

"No."

In Eli's darkened bedroom, the small green light from the stereo cast a reassuring governmental glow. It was, I imagined, the same dim luminescence tinting the faces of the two young soldiers in an underground bunker somewhere in eastern Montana, the ones I had once read about whose job it was to watch the screens for incoming nuclear threats while half a mile above them, antelope bedded down for the night in the long, end-of-summer grass.

Back in the big city in Eli's room, I smiled. My dilated eyes wandered over the rectangles of photos on the wall, the bookcase, the dresser. I picked out my backpack in the corner, which looked hewn and monumental. I cleared my throat.

"He told Pavia, 'Eli's a weird little fucker, but he thinks Thea's the cat's ass.'"

They only ever talked about it once, Walter and Judith. It was when Walter had been working for Judith for ten years or so. He had recently moved out of our family's house into the little farmhouse down the street from the library. It was summer. He was sitting at the kitchen table, smoking and reading while moths pelted the light fixture in a stupid and dusty compulsion overhead.

Walter lowered the book onto its face. He pushed back from the table and stood up. He hitched up the back of his jeans with one hand and reached for the phone with the other. He dialed Judith's house.

Her dog was barking in the background as she picked up. "Standish," Judith had said. "Do you mind?"

Walter liked the way she talked to the dog—not in a baby voice, not yelling—but with an appealing weariness. Whatever he said after this point—not that he knew what he was going to say, or even why he had picked up the phone in the first place—he had heard in her voice that she wouldn't be shocked that he had called.

"It's me. Walter." Walter said. "Just wondering what you're up to."

She'd been doing laundry. Reading, too—a new book about a songbird facing extinction; some people were trying to bring it back. There was a wildlife preserve but the birds weren't mating or the eggs didn't survive; no one knew exactly what was failing. They talked about that for a while and agreed to trade books in a few days.

"We could have coffee at 3Bee's before work," Walter said. "It's near my new place."

"New place?"

Walter told her that he had moved out. He said that Dorothy had problems. "I couldn't take it anymore," he told Judith. "I know that's shitty."

"Standish," Judith warned her dog again, who had started growling. "Not necessarily, no. You have to save yourself first, right?"

"I guess," Walter said. He gave a bitter little laugh, the kind you read about. "But it's not like I'm going back in to save anybody else."

"Who could you save?" Judith asked. "Not Dorothy. Not the girls."

226

"Why not the girls?"

"They're girls." There was a small silence. "Teenagers."

"Too late, then?"

"For what?" She didn't wait for an answer, "You love them. You'll see them. That's enough." Walter could imagine her shutting a book, putting it on the bookcart, moving down the middle aisle of the library; she was pulling the cart slowly along behind her with one hand like someone walking an old dog, someone leading a young child, someone pulling a wheeled suitcase.

"Maybe," Walter said. "But it doesn't feel like enough." He listened to Judith breathing into the receiver. Walter stepped forward and pressed his face into the screen door; he could smell the tang of aluminum and the cool air straining through it. The yellow moon shone on the patchy spider grass in his backyard, and the crickets thrummed like the night's heartbeat.

"I know," Judith said after a while. "I know it. Nothing feels like enough."

Nothing is enough. Walter heard her words with a slow sense of recognition, like something peeling open. And this hurt so much, so directly, that he could hardly breathe. He let his body lean deeper into the screen; the little wires crossed against the flesh of his cheek, digging in. He closed his eyes. And when he closed his eyes two hot tears came out; they were the only tears he could remember having shed in his life. And for no good reason.

"Walter?" Judith's voice was alive as skin against him, and his tears came quicker then, hotter. "Walter? Hello?"

He took a small breath, all he could manage. "Fine," he said into the receiver, but it was a gasp. Then he wanted so much not to make another sound like that gasp.

"Walter?" she asked. "Should I come over?" Every time she spoke it hurt—but not enough. Judith was right. Nothing was going to be enough. Not pain, not good things. "Walter," she was asking, "Should I?'

"No," he said. It was his teeth that were speaking, but he found he could breathe a little now. He took two more breaths. "I appreciate it. Judith. But no."

A car crept down the alley behind Walter's backyard and stopped a few houses down. The car door opened and slammed; someone yelled *later!* The car drove off, gravel popping and crunching beneath its wheels; the beams of its headlights swung past and away like heavy things.

Walter and Judith said goodnight; he hung up the phone. He smoked another cigarette, sitting at the table and staring at the crossword. Then he went to his room and lay down on his bed. He waited for sleep to erase him, and it did.

The next time they spoke on the phone outside of work was years later. Again, it was a summer night. Judith called him; she was sick.

"It was either call you or call my ex-husband," she told him with a frightened and therefore girlish laugh. "Please come."

Judith lived two streets over in a yellow house that glowed faintly under the streetlamp like a Post-it note. Walter knocked once at the door and then opened it. He walked through the front room to the hall, then to her bedroom. The door was slightly open and he pushed it forward.

The first thing he saw was Judith's hair on a Styrofoam head on the bedside table. The head's smooth, egg-like face was like something deleted. Judith, who was sitting in bed, raised her head from her bent knees and looked at him.

And she was beautiful. Her gray eyes were large and clear. And with its dents and asymmetries covered in a fine gray down, her head was as singular and perfect as a drop of smoky glass.

Walter moved toward Judith with an outstretched hand,

and his yellow fingers reached for the phone. He began to call the ambulance. His eyes were burning as he looked at her. He knew she was going to die—that she was on her way, in fact—and he was going to watch.

He wasn't surprised. He felt, instead, a sense of fullness, as if by sharing in a disappointment so complete it was a kind of fullness.

It was almost enough.

Judith was breathing through her mouth and then she began to cough. He put the phone receiver down on the table and held her head as she coughed, and kissed her skull, feeling in his lips and hands how—like a book or the subject of a book—she exceeded herself.

33. YOU MAY SURPRISE YOURSELF

If you would like a dog, we'll have to talk. I really wouldn't want a small dog, a nervous one that pees on the floor when you yell at it, or trembles, or barks too much and usually at stupid things—the ceiling fan, the vacuum—or one that wants to sleep on your bed, or one that smells dirty or is dirty, one that growls at other dogs, or humps legs and small children and soccer balls or adults crouched down to tie their shoes, or takes too long to find a place to shit, or one that sheds, an underfoot-type of dog that trips you constantly, or one that never learns to sit or do a trick, one that whines and cries and needs you too much, or one that doesn't discriminate. Shoves his wet-leather nose into your hand or your crotch all the time, whoever you may be.

Still, if you want one like that—if you really love it for some reason, acutely—then, okay.

34. THE SNAILS

And when Walter left the big city, we noticed that it was also the end of summer again. After work, the sun lapsed quickly behind the buildings; the cold sprang into place. The streets around the world famous university were suddenly infused, one weekend, with a stream of unparkable minivans. The sidewalks clogged with people, tables of book bags and day planners, discarded flyers for Chinese buffets. With Jack and Pavia and Xavier installed in the townhouse and me at Eli's, the end of that summer felt important and serious, almost Soviet, as if we had completed one years-long plan and were about to embark on another.

And so we were. Eli suddenly got a poorly paid but nevertheless real job, teaching photography (and juggling, guitar, and basic chess) at an alternative school called Sunny Dale. He was replacing a teacher who went to an ashram in New Jersey and had failed to come back.

For my part, I went to the doctor. I wanted to learn why, in months of determined, frequent coitus—during which my daily basal temperatures were noted and recorded, my cervical mucus faithfully cat's cradled between thumb and forefinger—sex alone wasn't doing the trick.

My doctor didn't know why. I was instead referred to a reproductive endocrinologist. This specialist looked at my hairy forearms and made a note in my chart.

"Any problems controlling your temper?" he asked smoothly.

His Adam's apple moved up and down inside his tanned neck like something you should reach in and pull out like a ripcord.

I knew what he suspected. He suspected I couldn't get pregnant because, hormonally speaking, I was too much a man, not woman enough. *The story of my life*, I thought—to be excessive and insufficient at the same time. I hated that doctor and I was ashamed. I declined his offer of further testing; I was resistant to treatment.

Thus I didn't become pregnant for my birthday that year, or for Thanksgiving or Christmas. Spring arrived with its usual grotesque displays—fat tulips, Frisbee games—and unlike the rest of the natural world, I did not manage to bring forth new life.

"I'd like to run some tests," the endocrinologist once again affirmed. I wanted not to submit to testing, not to know, to persist in noncompliance.

"I want to go to New York," Eli said at breakfast.

"You should, for the weekend," said Cassandra, eagerly, over coffee.

I shrugged. I had been so tired lately. I was twenty-six, almost twenty-seven, each minute older than I had ever been before, and feeling it.

The problem was, I wasn't sleeping well. In the early mornings, I would listen to Eli smack his lips in his sleep; Eli was what his dentist called a tongue thruster. All that summer I would lie awake next to him (Eli, not the dentist), sweating, imagining the wrong hormones streaming through my system, listening to his mouth. From time to time I'd give him an elbow jab to get him to turn over, facing away from me. And when the anemic light of early morning outlined the curtains, I would finally sit up, locate the floor with my feet, and head for the kitchen to start coffee.

Once the coffee began to brew, I would open the kitchen door and step into the small backyard. There, for the first time in my life and in a sad and half-acknowledged rite of fertility, I had planted flowers. The neighbor's pitbull, Knuckles, chained to his plywood doghouse, would go apeshit with joy for my company.

But the snails, the snails! Symmetrical and cozy, little cinnamon rolls rolling over the grass and into my flowerbeds. Their tasteful neutral colors, their naturalness. Their feelers waving languidly, like parade balloons with their lengthy anchoring filaments, miming *we are friends of children everywhere*. The snails.

Squatting on my haunches, I would pincer each one up, index finger and thumb. The snail's soft body—moist and ruffle-edged—would relinquish its embrace with a soft and familiar mouth noise, then withdraw inside its shell. I would huck the snail over the fence. I would listen—ear cartilage metaphorically inclined, tongue pulsing over lower teeth—for the wet smack of its shell on the asphalt parking lot next door. Then I would look at Knuckles, now standing like a coffee table with his legs spread wide, peeing furiously. And where that snail had come from: a glistening silver trail across the leaves and loam, dead-ended.

At work Charmaine told me that if you smashed snails you released their sacks of snail eggs. You actually speed up the reproductive process, she told me, by killing them the way I was doing.

Charmaine's mother is a master gardener. She'd been married three times, to men with boats and golf club memberships. She'd produced a daughter each time. Charmaine's mother, I didn't doubt, had given her this fact about the snails along with other occult feminine knowledge such as how to care for linen, how to keep silver from tarnishing, and how to seem interested in golf. "What's your favorite recipe for peaches?" Charmaine had once asked me, the first summer I'd worked for her. I had stared back at her. It seemed clear that I was never going to be a person who has favorite recipes.

Maybe it was the hormones. Anyway, I kept on smashing the snails. My flowerbed—a tangle of idiot-proof larkspur, cosmos, and poppies, snail-scarred but nevertheless vigorous—thrashed in slow motion toward the sun. And I continued to fail to get pregnant.

I was thinking again of Dorothy, who, by the time she was my age had gotten pregnant easily, accidentally, twice. I'd been thinking of her at Pavia's wedding, too, when I was new to sexual activity myself, and before I realized all that it transmits (sex, I mean) and what heritable tendencies toward fear and sadder magic the two of us—Pavia and I—sheltered within ourselves as a result of Dorothy's improbable congress with our dad. I thought we were different from our mother, I mean.

The reception for Pavia and Jack's wedding had been held outside, under a white canopy on the back lawn of the Methodist church in Supernal. Dorothy was wearing ugly boxlike sunglasses, the ones that look like welder's goggles painted black. *They're in style and anti-cataract*, my mother claimed. Her pudgy hand shook as she lifted a plastic cup of wine to her mouth.

No one was talking to her. Walter was slowly pacing the area behind the church dumpsters, smoking. From time to time, I would hug my mother from behind—a cheery half-nelson—and when she turned around (a three-point turn here, my mother taking tiny concubine steps to shift her point of view), I would already be moving away into the crowd. I would be floating off in my special dress, which I genuinely loved, in contradiction of the usual complaint of bridesmaids everywhere. Yes, by the time my mother turned around, the feel of my elbow still on her neck—I'd be gone.

And I thought of this: my mother with someone from the bar, in the dark, his body against hers. My mother's thrilled whispers, high-pitched, baby-talk.

For my twenty-seventh birthday, we rode the train to New York. It was my first trip there. We stayed in the East Village, in the empty apartment of one of Eli's friends. The apartment was like a dark shoebox, with one small window that opened onto an airshaft. We walked around a lot, going in and out of shops so small and coherently decorated I began to feel oppressed. The salesgirls, blank as emery boards in their sleek outfits, ignored us. On a sudden defensive impulse, I insisted we go to the museum, the Metropolitan.

For several hours, I walked behind Eli through the wings of the Met, becoming increasingly aware, on the miles of hard flooring, that I was engaged in a weight-bearing activity, one that would, with luck, stave off osteoporosis for a few minutes in fifty years. As a person lacking the bone-protective effects of endocrine balance—not to mention pregnancy and lactation—the thought was mildly soothing to me. But my feet were killing me.

In the last half hour before the museum closed, we went into the cafeteria. This cafeteria, as you'll one day see for yourself, is an immense room, tall with columns and skylights, with sad and classy arcs of leaded glass above. Here we got a pot of tea—we ought to drink more tea, Eli and I impulsively agreed—and sat down at a table with our tray.

At the next table was a German couple, younger than us,

with good skin and neck scarves suggesting political engagement. Matching green backpacks sat on the floor next to their sturdy shoes. I felt myself leaning toward them. I pressed the teacup to my lips, pretending to blow.

How the Germans gazed into each other's eyes through their serious but not unflattering pairs of glasses! How in touch with life they seemed, with the war-like urgency of their conversation, their glottal stops and throaty vowels.

Motes of silver dust waltzed through the sunlight falling down on their table, and on ours.

"Are we going to get married?" I heard myself ask Eli.

I looked quickly at him, and I saw his eyes fill up, brighten.

"Are you proposing to me?" he asked.

"No." My throat closed down around the word. The panic that I felt was as slow as literature, hope-filled. No! If this were what I wanted, I wanted him to ask me. It should be natural, unassisted; I should be the girl.

And then, like the Germans next to us, our hands were clasped on top of a marble table, our fingers full of each other's fingers holding tight on either side of the institutional teapot. Eli swallowed.

"Maybe you're not asking," he said, eyelashes glistening now with unshed tears, "But I'm getting a hard on."

Eli bought me a ring in the museum gift shop that day, and it wasn't long before the skin under the band was paler than the rest, like a perforation separating us from before. When I typed at work, or washed the dishes at home, or reached out for Xavier during our Sunday dinners at Pavia and Jack's house, I liked to see the ring there on my hand. I liked the green plaque that eventually grew in its hammered crevices; I liked its stalwart, Old World shine. It was as if it had been in the family for generations, as if the generations were a wise and kindly group looking down on me from their sepia-toned heaven.

Instead there was Dorothy calling late at night, reading aloud from her new book on vitamins.

"E is good for your hair," she would tell me, "It's good for your eyes."

"Everyone knows that," I said, moving the basal thermometer to the other side of my mouth.

"I know it," she said. She took a drag on her cigarette; smoking is one of her episodic habits, like phone calling and pressured speech. "But not *just* that." Her voice was like a leak in a tire as she exhaled—steady, hushed, urgent—"*Longevity*."

"Uh-huh," I said.

"But Thea. Thea! Also *fertility*."

I was lying in bed; it was very early in the morning. Eli was dreaming beside me, warm and material. My mother read on and on into my ear, Chapter Three of *E: The Miracle Vitamin*. I thought of her words thrusting across the pillow and moving out into the black backyard, little helmets advancing on the foliage, a war of the nighttime world. I put my hand on Eli's narrow back. He smacked his lips and said in his sleep, "Sleep. Go to sleep. Baby, go to sleep."

35. IN WHICH THE RADIO MAKES ME CRY

The road to you has a dotted line down the middle. It's all the white sticks I've peed on, all the home pregnancy tests with their pairs of lavender lines. These are the minus signs, the double negatives.

The road is the road I drove with Dorothy next to me and the animal that I killed on the pavement behind us.

The road shimmers in the heat like the start of a dream sequence; it's the highway that my father drives with Judith in the passenger's seat; she's reading aloud from a book.

Pavia drove this road when she left Xavier; she had gotten lost.

It's the road between Supernal and our big city. It crosses seven states. Along this road everything changes; the mountains fall back and the farmland comes up, then the lakes—green to gold to blue—and at last there are small cities and then our city.

Along the way the radio plays and plays. And just when the chorus of the song is about to start—the verse is over and you're in the bridge, the drummer kicks it up a notch and everything inside you suddenly wants to hurry forward or bear down hard—the station burns away, sizzling off like something on a hot pan. It's suddenly behind you, overhead, and gone.

36. A CAMEO APPEARANCE

Eli came to Montana with me for Christmas that year. We stayed with my dad, sleeping in his bed while he took the couch. One day on the way back from the grocery store with Eli, I decided to drive past the house I'd grown up in. I took a right at Supernal's last stoplight before the mountains, crossed the railroad tracks, and headed up the shallow canyon at the end of which lay what we had always, without affection, called *our development*.

Dorothy's house had been sold to a home-schooling Christian family with four young boys. I imagined the cleaning they must have had to do: before her move to Supernal Manor, Dorothy had quit housework completely, including taking the garbage out. I thought too of the home decorating that the young family might have undertaken recently: stenciled fruits at the top of the kitchen walls, for example, and quilted cozies on the toaster and blender. Toilet lids with flower decals. All the unnecessary domestic ornament that Pavia and I had lately learned to scorn but secretly still wanted or at least felt fond of, like the relative you never had. Maybe the house looked good now, maybe it was working for them?

The snow was piled up in dirty banks on either side of the street as Eli and I slowly drove past the house like burglars making the neighborhood. We silently noted the similar ranch-style houses in sage green or clay or sunset—ours alone still surrounded by dried weeds poking up in tufts under the windows—and all the domestically manufactured cars in the driveways. We saw the vapors rising from the aluminum vents on the roofs, two deer springing over a chain link fence and flashing off through the backyards toward the mountains. And the pang I felt as we crept along wasn't nostalgia; it was relief. I was never coming back.

The alert reader may ask, "What is Supernal Manor?" and/ or "What became of Dorothy?" or yet even, "Otherwise, shouldn't Eli and Thea have stayed at Dorothy's home during this trip to Montana, rather than the too-small residence of Walter?"

In fact, Supernal Manor was the assisted-living facility to which Pavia and Jack had had to move Dorothy. In this move, thankfully, I did not directly participate. I did, however, call my mother soon afterward.

The ringing of Dorothy's new phone line had a flat, insectal buzz—a corporate sound. She picked up on the second ring.

"Hi," I said. "It's me," I said, then added, "Thea."

"Darling," she said.

I asked as many of the usual questions as I could think of—Was her room comfortable? How was the food? Did the people seem nice?—but there weren't many of those.

"The other residents are...nice," Dorothy said slowly. "They're all pretty old." We observed a moment of silence for them, the other residents. I could see them perfectly, which is to say I could imagine them well, as they sat at the round tables in the dining hall, kyphosis hooking their necks forward till their faces—rough, whiskered, root-like—hung mere inches above their plastic placemats.

"Do they tell you where to sit?" I asked suddenly. "In the dining hall I mean, do you have to decide who to sit with at each meal, or are there assigned seats, or...?"

"Oh," my mother said. "No. No, they tell you."

"Oh! That's good." I nodded stupidly, for emphasis. I was holding the phone receiver to the side of my warm head; the cartilage of the top of my right ear bent back over the stem of my glasses. I was walking back and forth in the front room of Eli and Cassandra's house.

"So?" I said at last. "You're feeling okay? About the move?"

"What?" My mother sniffed: it was allergies or a cold, a medication side effect or part of a small sob. "What do you mean?" she asked.

"I'm sorry," I said. I said it louder. "I'm *sorry.*"

"What?" she said. "What?" And then she made a noise that was so much like a laugh; I sat down on the coffee table and listened. She went on.

"Darling, what for?" she said. "No. I have you and your sister; I have Walter." I was looking down at my bare feet on the wood floor, my dirty soles turned in like a tailor's; I was listening to each syllable stitch its way across the wires to me. "Darling," my mother—your grandmother—said, "What more could I want? I have you."

In Supernal, Eli was enthusiastic about the abundance of pawnshops. We spent the morning of Christmas Eve walking from one to the other in the small streets near the railroad station, flipping through boxes of 8-track tapes and old *Playboy* magazines. Eli bought a ukulele for Xavier and a dusty case of discontinued film for the Brownie cameras he used with his students. And in one shop, nestled in a slit in a black velvet display tray, I found my cameo ring. This was the ring that had been Alva's and then promised to me, but pawned or stolen or lost when Dorothy came to the big city, three years earlier.

I bought the ring, of course. I renewed my affection for its ugliness—on a chapped-looking background of pink carnelian, it featured the profile of an anonymous lady with a Hapsburg underbite—and it fit me perfectly. I wore it nearly every day of that Christmas holiday in Supernal. I was wearing it when Eli and I went with Walter to the cemetery to visit Judith's grave.

The cemetery was on a little square of land that used to be on the edge of town. Supernal had since grown and sprawled around it; now there were houses on three sides and a string of small businesses—a taco place, a gun place, a fabric shop, a convenience store—on the other side. The green Kwik In n' Out sign faced the metal cutout letters, SUPERNAL CITY CEMETERY, arranged in an arch over the entrance.

The three of us drove slowly on the muddy road that wound through the cemetery. It was a warm day; the snow slid off the pine tree boughs in clumps that spattered apart when they hit the ground. We drove to the back of the cemetery, stopped the car. We got out and walked to Judith's grave. Water shone in between the letters of her name on the small metal plate sticking up out from the ground.

My father leaned over and put a bouquet of daisies on the ground next to the plate. The plastic was still wrapped around the flowers; the afternoon light flashed off the cellophane and snow. I listened to Walter's quiet wheezing as I stood there.

"I wish I'd met her," Eli said. "What was she like?"

My father cleared his throat. A small plane buzzed overhead with an unsure, archival sound. I looked up and saw the dark outline of a person in a stand of pine trees near the entrance to the cemetery. I shaded my eyes with a mittened hand; the person was waving. As he moved through the mud and snow toward us, I saw that it was Joseph.

Leaving Eli and Walter at the grave, I walked over to meet him. As Joseph got closer I saw his sunburned face seemed to have sunk in slightly, like a failed cake.

"Hey girlie!" He had a sleeping bag on his back, and gave me a one-armed hug. "*Suuntsaa!*" He stepped back and smiled proudly at me.

"*Suuntsaa* yourself. D'Agostino? You're not Indian." I had looked at my high school yearbook: Joseph d'Agostino. Art club. JV basketball.

Joseph smiled slowly, showing his teeth and his missing teeth. "Viva Italia. Is that Eli? That your dad?" I nodded. I explained that we were visiting the grave of Walter's boss.

"No way. That lady at the library, you mean? Judith?" Joseph asked. "Black-brown hair, kind of...," he moved his hand about his head in an imaginary shampoo.

"Right," I said, nodding. "Wig, I'm pretty sure."

"She was a good lady. If you fell asleep in the library, she wouldn't wake you up. She'd let you stay all day."

"How about him?" I inclined my head toward Walter. He was still at the graveside talking to Eli. I wished I could hear what he was saying; I was missing the story. "What's my dad's reputation at the library?"

Joseph shrugged. "I don't know. I don't hang out there much now. How's Dorothy?"

I told him about the assisted living place; he nodded. "Good. That's good. She'll be safe there. No one to try and take advantage of her, you know?"

I looked at him. What was there to say?

"You know? Thea? Safe?"

Now it was my turn to nod. "She's really down at the moment. Like, can't-get-out-of-bed down."

"Yeah." Joseph shifted the rope that held his sleeping bag to the other shoulder. "Yep," he said.

Strings of yarn got caught on the cameo ring as I pulled off my mitten. I worked them free and held out my hand to Joseph.

"Getting married!" Joseph said, "Congratulations!"

"Oh. Well. Actually, it's the ring you and Mom pawned three years ago. Remember? It's my ring, the one my grandmother saved for me. We found it and bought it back."

He wiped his nose on the back of his hand as he looked down at the ring. He broke into a huge smile. "Cool. You've got good luck, Thea."

I smiled back into his happy, ruining face. I considered for a moment my luck. I looked back over my shoulder at where Walter and Eli still stood together at the grave. My father had his head down and was coughing into the collar of his wool coat—or else, impossibly, he was crying. Just then Eli looked up at me, and it was like a pocket mirror flashing the sun, signaling *here*.

"Luck." I found my wallet in my coat pocket and slid out a twenty. I pulled the ring off my finger and handed it with the cash to Joseph.

"Good luck to you," I said. I held my breath as I kissed him on the cheek and turned away. I walked a few feet back toward the grave, then turned back. Joseph was already heading toward the entrance.

"Hey Joseph?" I pulled off my other mitten and held up my left hand, Eli's ring on my finger, as he turned around. "But I am getting married!"

His remaining teeth shone white in his mouth. He waved, turned, and kept on walking, his feet smudging a bluish trail in the snow.

37. THE HEART IS A FIST-SHAPED MUSCLE

The carpet-cleaning salesman on the phone doesn't know my name. Is this Mrs. Greathouse? Is this Mrs. James?

I'm not helping. *Nope. No*, I say, *Afraid not.*

Exasperated, he tries again, "Well, are you the mommy?"

And he has interrupted my new favorite daydream: I am walking my infant daughter in the park. A stranger bends down to look at her in her stroller and gasps, draws back, horrified...! For there among the flannel a half-formed twin grows out of my baby's shoulder, wriggling like a handpuppet.

Or else my baby's arms and legs are shortened, smooth as melted candles, no hands and feet.

Or perhaps she has only one large eye in the middle of her smooth forehead.

Yes. One eye, big and brown, fringed by long black lashes. A shiny eye in the middle of her pink forehead, above her button nose and rosebud mouth. An eye that opens and smiles out like the great I AM of Sunday school banners, the fat-bellied dove of PAX looking mildly on... The big eye that sees me, the new mother, flying through the air like a human fork (the least comforting of the flatware) toward the strange man still more aghast, the eye that sees me stab, wrench, pull, then lunge forward and slug the man, hitting him again and again until I (*Mommy!*) switch to kicking as the man goes down, teeth tumble-washing in a mouth of bright and briny blood, terrified of the two of us and completely uncomprehending. *Two on one!*

This daydream makes my heart feel flushed and tender, like a well-used fist that surges up, up, up—and connects.

"Then are you the homeowner?" the carpet salesman on the phone finally asks.

I smile, pull the elastic waistband lower on my newly widened hips, the pelvic cradle. I say, "No, I'm the mom."

38. IN WHICH I APOLOGIZE FOR MY MATERIAL

Today my Bishop score—the clinical measure of cervical ripeness—is eleven. I'm ready. I'm like a rubber jar today, upended and distended. I feel your weight in my mouth—the other one—as you curl there in it, waiting.

You're past due but don't worry: you're not really late. I've needed the extra time even after all the time trying to get pregnant, all the gynecologic rummaging by others' cold (if expert) hands, all the medication and artificial hormones that I agreed to introduce and then abandoned, all our laughter when I got knocked up anyway eventually, despite my many flaws. I wanted time to write down some things for you, and I had to do it now—before I cease to be myself and start becoming yours.

Some advice. Some medical history. Some back story. A kind of excuse.

I only made it to the part of the story where your dad and I decided to stay together and have a baby, maybe you. It took years by the way, during which we did eventually marry. We had the wedding at the chapel at Sunny Dale, where your dad teaches. It was fall, an afternoon. Beforehand, by the girl's bathroom sink,

Cassie dressed me in a long green gown that fell around my legs like a new husk; by eight that evening she had met and fallen in love with the (unmarried) school chaplain. They have three little girls now, all named after flowers, and they live in a school-owned house at the cemetery's edge.

Dorothy was there at the wedding, beaming impersonally at me from the front row. Walter was there too, his oxygen tank hissing quietly on the bench between them. Xavier was there wearing his Star Wars watch upside-down on his wrist, occasionally clutching his penis through his dress pants. Jack sat beside him with his arm across the back of the pew. Only your aunt Pavia was missing. She was sick that day. Her illness—stuck inside her like a lyric (specific, personal, far too interesting)—prevented her attendance.

Oh my daughter, my little simile! I'm sorry for the chromosomes that I gave to you. But it's only half the story, isn't it? Maybe less.

Yesterday your father and I were walking in the fields behind the school. The wind brushed through the long grasses by the water; they sighed and turned over, the blades twisting around each other like the reaching arms of a helix before splitting apart again. The undersides were paler green, unfinished.

You rolled and flexed against your father's hand pressed into my side, then settled down again exactly as before. *Madam, I'm Adam.*

Sometimes, when two people love each other very much, they want to get closer. I'm ready. So now, my girl: come closer.

ACKNOWLEDGMENTS

Portions of this novel first appeared, in slightly different versions, in *Western Humanities Review* and *PANK*.

I owe many thanks to Susan Anderson for her encouragement, wit, and help in every phase of this project. (Everyone should have a friend who spends her days in the basement reading poems about death.)

I'm also profoundly indebted to Shen Christenson, who read this manuscript over and over again, who helped shape and sharpen it, who showed me what I meant and helped me say it better. She edited this book like a mother—with huge heart, deep intelligence, and absolute commitment.

Gerda Saunders, beautiful writer and person, inspired and guided this book in every way I can think of. I'm very humbly grateful; this book simply wouldn't exist without her.

I thank the AWP for sponsoring the Award Series for the Novel and to Supriya Bhatanagar, Sarah Flood, and the rest of the AWP staff for their work on behalf of writers and readers. I particularly thank Steve Amick, who first saw merit in my manuscript, and Don Lee, who selected it for the award.

I'm also thankful to Kim Kolbe and New Issues Press, and to Keir Graff and Fingers Murphy for their wise guidance in the publishing process and for their support and good humor throughout.

I'm grateful to the Utah Arts Council's Original Writing Competition and to judge Michelle Latiolais for providing meaningful encouragement at exactly the right time.

Finally, I thank many other dear friends, relatives, and colleagues who have provided help, encouragement, childcare, anecdotes, sympathies, and indulgences during the time this book was written, reworked, and fretted over—especially the appealingly neurotic and uncommonly generous Tracy Vayo.

AWP Award Series in the Novel

Photo by Sean Graff

Kirstin Scott's stories have appeared in *Alaska Quarterly Review*, *Hayden's Ferry Review*, *Sonora Review*, *Western Humanities Review*, *PANK*, and elsewhere. She lives in Salt Lake City, Utah. *Motherlunge* is her first novel.